Praise for *The R...*

'She wrote ... makes you wo ... weeks ... the story has mystery-thriller suspense as well as several intriguing depths ... terrifically impressive'
The Independent

'An assured tone and decidedly bold denouement –
a talent to watch' *Financial Times*

'A compelling, impressive tale' *The Times*

'Ingenious and provocative exploration of faith,
fact and fantasy. Put it in your suitcase'
Hampstead & Highgate Express

'A skilful portrait of a man's inner turmoil' *Good Housekeeping*

'Hamand aims at more than a tricksy re-telling of an old
tale ... miracle and science, truth and myth, clash and
interweave in the raw glare of modernity' *Catholic Herald*

'A whodunnit, a ghost story, an original treatment of the crisis-
of-faith theme – even, as the tale comes to its uncomfortable
close, a full-blooded horror story' *Coventry Evening Telegraph*

'This is just one of those books you don't want to put down'
Lancashire Evening Telegraph

'Hamand creates a remarkable tension between the strong
sense of place and "ordinary life" and the mystery, the
uncertainty of mind and spirit. This is a truly crafty game with
the mystery/crime genre – post-modernism meets the Creed'
Sara Maitland

'Her work is outstanding – taut and tightly structured with a
wonderful narrative drive' Kathy Lette, LBC radio

'A rattling good read' Richard Chartres, Bishop of London

ALSO BY MAGGIE HAMAND

The Rocket Man

The Resurrection *of the* BODY

MAGGIE HAMAND

MAIA

First paperback edition
published in 2008 by
The Maia Press Limited
82 Forest Road
London E8 3BH
www.maiapress.com

ISBN 978 1 904559 30 6

A CIP catalogue record for this book is available
from the British Library

Printed and bound in Great Britain by Thanet Press
on paper from sustainable managed forests

The Maia Press is supported by Arts Council England

Author's Note

The Resurrection of the Body was originally written during a competition held in London in March 1994 to write a novel in 24 hours under examination conditions. It was the outright winner of the World One-Day Novel Cup, and the original version, just 23,000 words long, was published with the two runners-up by Images Publishing within 48 hours of their receiving the winning manuscripts. The novel was then expanded to almost twice that length for publication by Michael Joseph in 1995.

In expanding it, I left alone the existing text, just adding here and there where necessary and correcting any errors. Twenty-one chapters in this book are therefore much as they were written for the competition, while eighteen are completely new. One reason why I chose to expand the book this way was that I was anxious to keep the sparse style and narrative drive which seemed to be a product of the intense pressure under which the original version was written.

While all the locations in this book are real, including the parish church of St Michael and All Angels, London Fields, the characters are purely imaginary. However, I would like to take this opportunity to thank all those people who helped me in my researches and generously gave up their time and expertise to make the details in this book as realistic as possible.

Maggie Hamand, 2008

The Interruption in the Church

It was Good Friday, shortly after one o'clock, in the middle of the three-hour devotional service. The reading had just ended and the church was in perfect silence as we prayed. It was so still and calm that you could hear the background hum of traffic and the distant crying of a child. I looked down at the bowed heads of the diverse congregation, both black and white; the smart, middle-class professionals who had moved into the attractive Victorian housing in the area, the old East Enders like Sidney who had been born in the terrace a hundred yards away and still remembered the bomb falling on the house next door when he was only six, the black women from the grim estate round the corner.

My thoughts were interrupted by the sound of raised voices in the street. At first I took no notice of the disturbance. I could hear shouting, rough voices, and then someone starting to yell quite near us, right outside the church. Looking back, it was obvious that there was a great deal of distress in that voice, and had I put my prayers aside and acted then I might have been able to prevent what happened. In any case, I took no notice; in fact the sounds did not alarm but only irritated me, breaking as they did into my intense concentration, and I put them firmly to one side and withdrew back into my prayers.

The door at the back of the church banged and there was a scuffling in the vestibule. I looked up and my eye caught that of Chris Shaw, a local author who was one of the churchwardens; once before he had dealt very capably with a drunk who had wandered in from the pub round the corner during the middle of our confirmation service. He nodded to me, as if to say 'If it gets any worse I will go and deal with it.' Then came a sound which I shall never forget, a dreadful, powerful, bewildered cry; and through the open door came a man, lurching forward, staggering, holding his hands to his side.

I had never seen the colour of fresh blood before in such profusion, so bright, splashed everywhere, like scarlet paint. The man sank to the floor and we all rose to our feet at the same moment, like a wave. Somebody ran to the door and out on to the porch; someone else rushed to my office to use the phone. Chris's wife Anne, a doctor, was beside the man in an instant, calling out instructions;

I remember seeing all this and feeling paralysed, power-
less, unable to move.

My reaction shocked me. I have seen many terrible
things in my time, people suffering and dying, but this
was different, too violent and sudden; I didn't want to
have to look at this. There I had been, in prayer contemplating the wounds of Christ on the cross, but presented
with real wounds I was shivering with fear and ineptness.
I forced myself to cross the floor and kneel beside the
man. Anne was in charge; I asked her, 'Can I help you?'

Anne was pulling away the man's clothes, already
soaked in blood, and asking for something to cover the
wound. Someone came from the vestry with the linen and
handed it to her; Mercy was cutting into a tablecloth with
scissors. Anne told me it was important to sit him upright
and turn him to one side, because the lung was punctured
and he would have difficulty breathing, and that if he lay
flat he would probably choke. In an urgent whisper she
told me to support him leaning on one side so that blood
didn't flow from the injured lung into the good one. So I
knelt behind him, holding him awkwardly under his
shoulders, while they folded squares of linen and tore
strips to cover and bind the wound.

After this there was silence, because there was nothing
we could do. The ambulance was on its way; Mercy was
impatient, muttering, 'Oh Lord, why do they take so long?'
The man's face, as I looked down on it, was pale and
damp, sticky with sweat. He had an olive complexion,
which now took on a greenish tinge, almost the putty-

coloured look of a newborn baby, and his eyes were very dark. For a moment I couldn't help thinking of how close are the processes of birth and death. The man tried to say something, but I couldn't distinguish what it was, and when they asked me about it afterwards I was not even sure that it was English. This effort seemed too much for him; he began to cough up blood and a pale, frothy liquid appeared on his lips. His eyes dimmed and all his being seemed focused on the terrible struggle to draw breath. Anne, with her clinical detachment, was doing everything she could; one of the other women, Mary, patted his hand and talked soothingly to him as you would to a sick child. I blessed her for this. I myself could say nothing; I could only pray silently, and wait for the ambulance to come.

My arms began to ache with the strain of supporting the heavy body. Mary held his limp, pale hand within her own plump, dark ones, massaging it gently as if by doing so she could transfer some of her own warmth and energy into him. As she stroked his hand she turned it over and I saw that the blood which I had thought must have got there when he put his hand to his side came from a deep wound across the palm, as if it had been slashed or pierced with a knife.

Now, with intense relief, I heard the siren in the distance, then another out of tune with it, then a third, all steadily growing stronger. The police arrived first. I could hear their voices outside in the porch, and the ambulance came only a few seconds later. A voice behind me said, 'Please step aside, we'll deal with this now.' With relief I eased the man into a paramedic's arms; when I got to my feet I could see that my robes were brightly smeared with blood. I stood as if hypnotised, watching what they would do with him.

Their movements were quick, efficient, though they took their time, putting an oxygen mask to his face, inserting a drip into his arm, dressing the wound. They lifted him on to a stretcher and then, with a burst of fuss and movement, he was gone from the church. A shaft of sunlight suddenly pierced the air, shining through the stained glass below the roof and casting dappled patterns on the floor, lighting up the trail of blood. We heard the ambulance start and the siren fading swiftly as it roared away down the road.

The Police Ask Questions

My parish is in Hackney, in London Fields, one of the poorest boroughs in the country. The church is a miserable-looking building on the outside, dull red brick and all awkward lines and angles, and too many slabs of bare brick wall. But inside it is quiet and pale and cool, smooth cream plaster and a domed white roof, built on the Byzantine plan in the late 1950s by Cachemaille-Day.

On two sides of the square interior are six paintings depicting various Biblical scenes showing the intervention of angels. First there are Adam and Eve driven out of Eden and the angel with the flaming sword. Across the nave Jacob wrestles with the angel. Then come the four New Testament scenes; the annunciation, the nativity with

15

heavenly hosts, the agony in the garden of Gethsemane with the angel keeping watch, and the angel at the empty tomb.

In the centre of this calm space we all stood bewildered. How could we carry on the service after this? Even as I hesitated, wondering how best to proceed, one of the policemen took me by the elbow and indicated that we should step outside into the vestibule. He was very calm and polite; even the police seemed to understand that we had all been, as it were, in a trance – that it was not appropriate to ask the questions they needed to in the church, in the middle of a service.

I felt very strongly that I couldn't just abandon the congregation at this moment. I asked the others, while we were gone, to carry on, for the choir to sing the next hymn and Chris to do the reading. Then I followed the police sergeant outside into the vestibule.

I was shocked at first by the quantity of blood on the floor. It lay in irregular puddles, smeared here and there by dragging feet, and there was a trail running through into the church; I realised with horror that I had some on my shoes. There were several policemen standing there, looking nervous and uncomfortable, and outside, in the pale spring sunlight, I saw several cars parked across the road, their blue lights flashing. Police radios crackled noisily as they relayed incomprehensible messages. A few passers-by had stopped and were staring; the police were already beginning to put tape across the entrance to the church.

I led the sergeant into the room which we used as a crèche and sat down heavily on a chair.

I should say straight away that I do not have much trust in the police. Living where we do, I suppose that I tend to see the worst of them. Recently we had had a great deal of trouble with them, because they had come to the churchwarden Mercy's house with a warrant to arrest her son, who had been in trouble with the police over some petty crime. When Mercy said he was not there they had roughly pushed her aside and searched the house. In doing so they had broken or damaged some of her things, and in great distress she had left the house and come to see me. The police had followed her and, Mercy said, assaulted her. When she arrived at the vicarage she had broken glasses and a black eye. The police accused her of assaulting them and brought a charge against her (which had still to come to court). I had gone to see Detective Chief Inspector Stone at Stoke Newington Police Station and told him what I thought about the incident, that I knew that Mercy would never harm anyone, that she was our representative on the East London Deanery Synod and that people who would speak up for her would include the Bishop himself.

Perhaps this sergeant knew about this case because at first he seemed ill at ease; he wouldn't look me in the eyes and paid too much attention to his notebook. But whatever he may have been thinking initially he soon put to one side, and his manner became entirely businesslike.

He said they wanted to evacuate the church. There were certain things they needed to do, fingerprinting, looking for the weapon which might have been discarded, for any traces that might point to the identity of the attacker.

Police cars were out now in force, combing the streets, looking for anyone suspicious, and the police helicopter had been requested. First of all, he wanted to know if anyone had seen the man who carried out the assault. At this point one of the police constables put his head round the door and said that one man had run out into the street as soon as the victim had entered the church, but had seen no signs of anyone running away. We all said that we had seen no one. The sergeant made a note of this and said they needed access to the front of the church so that they could begin straight away. Of course it was a bank holiday weekend and this would cause some problems, but they needed to get a police photographer and the forensic people to work as soon as possible, though they might not be available until the next day. Meanwhile it was very important that the scene of the crime should not be disturbed.

I said that this would not be a problem, but urged them to be as quick as possible. Of course the church had to be prepared for our Easter services, and since the Easter Vigil began before dawn on Sunday, everything had to be ready the night before.

I was wondering if it would be their responsibility or ours to clean away the blood when they had finished.

The sergeant said he was sure everything could be done by then. He asked if there was any way the congregation could leave the church without coming through the vestibule and perhaps disturbing the evidence. I explained that there was another door, at the back, which led to my office and to the church hall. We agreed to evacuate the church and continue the service in the church hall. The police were happy for the service to continue but they wanted to talk to anyone who had heard anything, or might know the man who had been assaulted, and that it would be helpful if they did this as soon as possible.

I said that I was sure that nobody knew him. I had never seen him before myself. He had certainly never been a member of the congregation.

The sergeant continued his questioning in that mannered, precise way that policemen have. First he needed a description of the victim. How old was he?

I told him that it was hard to say. He had thick, dark hair, no trace of balding or greying, but his complexion was slightly battered, as if he had led an outdoor life. I guessed that he was in his early to mid-thirties. He had black eyes, a straight, if not slightly Roman nose and full lips. His skin was not quite white but not dark either, perhaps Middle Eastern, or southern European – Spanish, perhaps. But it was hard to say because of the extreme pallor caused by shock and loss of blood.

He tried to establish whether the assault had actually taken place in the vestibule, which seemed likely from the quantity of blood on the floor. I told him I had heard shouting in the street, only a minute or two before the man entered the church. I couldn't distinguish any words, but I had the feeling that it was English; yes, undoubtedly one of the men had a rough, East-End accent. The cry that he had given at the moment of the stabbing seemed to come from inside the vestibule. I added that the man himself had said nothing, he had tried to speak but no words had been distinguishable, and I couldn't say what language he had used. We had taken nothing out of his pockets, hadn't looked for any identification. I was sorry, there wasn't much more I could say.

Searching my mind for anything else that might be relevant, some little detail that might have escaped me or be of some importance, I mentioned the cut I had seen on the man's hand. I noticed something cross the sergeant's face then, a strange kind of expression, not a smile, exactly, nor a sneer. He made a note in his little black book. Mary, sitting behind me, said she had noticed there were cuts on both his hands. Again, he wrote this down, with a little flourish.

I cannot remember how long this questioning went on for; the police seemed to need everything repeated several times and kept asking for information which we didn't have. They said they would have to come back for formal statements. I tried to be patient. My main concern was for the man; I asked the sergeant where he had been taken and he said to Bart's. Anne, who had come in and was now standing behind me, said that though the injury was very serious she thought there was a good chance that he would survive if he reached the hospital alive.

The police said that it would make things a great deal easier for them if he was able to talk, and that they would want to talk to everyone again once they began to build up the investigation.

The sergeant suddenly stood up and snapped his notebook shut. 'Don't worry,' he said, 'We'll find whoever is responsible. We'll get to the bottom of this, I promise.'

I went through to the church hall. The choir were

singing, very simply and plainly, 'Glory be to Jesus in his bitter pain.' I tried to look deeply into my mind to understand what I was feeling. I felt sickened and repelled. Contemplating the suffering of Christ was not the same as contemplating the suffering of that man. Christ, we are told, comes back to life; that somehow renders his suffering more bearable. This man would not have the same hope. We are all terrified of death, none more so than myself. It was the look in that man's eyes which haunted me, that stricken look as if he recognised that this was the end of him and that there was nothing to be done about it. This knowledge struck through me as if I myself had been pierced with a knife. When I thought I had truly entered into a knowledge of suffering in my prayers, something real had stumbled across my path to say: This is a conceit. This is not so.

I sat at the front of the hall and listened to the choir's intense, quiet singing. Despite my attempts to listen, to return to the prayerful state in which I had begun this service, disturbing thoughts kept running through my head. Only yesterday an intelligent, middle-class woman had come to me saying she was disturbed by the erotic nature of Christ's passion. I understood at once what she meant; the same thing has from time to time troubled me. There are many erotic images of Christ on the cross, and the combination of art and death has many sexual overtones. But there is nothing erotic whatsoever in real suffering, only obscenity. Christ's death is not obscene because we give it meaning. In order to come to terms with death, surely every death must have a meaning.

I had to bring the service to a close. I spoke briefly, saying that what had happened today had profoundly shocked us. Words, I said, were inadequate; but we could also express ourselves in silence. We were silent, then, for perhaps five minutes. Then I said the blessing, and the service ended. We filed slowly out of the hall; nobody said anything to me. The choir followed me into my office, as did Tessa, the deaconess. We said a quick prayer together, and then embraced one another. Tessa in particular seemed dreadfully upset, and I could see tears glittering in her eyes. She put her arms around me and we held one another closely for a moment, giving and receiving comfort.

We went outside. Police vans blocked the road and there were policemen everywhere taping off the area; a small crowd gathered on the pavement. The sun had gone in, the sky darkened and a few drops of chill rain fell.

Above us, roaring in the sky, was the familiar sight and sound of the police helicopter. I stood in the road and watched it circling overhead, the sound of its rotors uncomfortably loud. The police cars were leaving; after a while the helicopter too drifted away towards the East.

A policeman came and asked me to help lock up the church. They asked for the keys so that they could have access when the forensic people came. I said that they could get a set now from one of the churchwardens, but they were free to ask me at any time. I locked up the church, and they left a policeman standing guard at the door.

✝he Accusations Begin

Harriet was waiting for me at the entrance to the vicarage. She had heard what had happened, and her face was tense and anxious. I walked into the kitchen. I could hear the children running round upstairs; their voices sounded very distant and otherwise the house was in silence. My wife put on the kettle. Its hissing and gurgling sounded unnaturally loud after the silence of the church; I looked out into the garden and watched the daffodils dancing in the cold wind.

Harriet looked at me and asked, in her quiet, understanding way, 'Do you want to tell me about it?'

I said, 'Later.' I took the cup of tea that she had made and retreated into the dining room.

Almost immediately the doorbell rang. I closed my eyes; I wasn't sure that I could face anyone just now. Harriet came to the door and said that it was Sidney, a member of our congregation, and that he wanted to speak to me urgently. I said that I would see him for ten minutes.

Sidney lives just a few streets away from us in a flat in the house where he was born; as a child he endured the worst of the Blitz, and he had often recounted his experiences to me. He looked very awkward and ill at ease in my study in his baggy, crumpled clothes. He looked at the paintings on the walls and the photos on my desk, staring round at this, what must have seemed to him, extraordinary luxury. Sidney's flat, which I had visited, was small and dreary, and he had hardly any possessions. Although we were by no means rich, I was so often made to feel uneasy about my comfortable, middle-class lifestyle when so many of my congregation were so poor.

He said, in a deep voice, 'I think I know who done it.'

'What?' I hadn't expected this, and was startled out of the feeling of apathy which had overcome me. 'Who?'

'That nutter, Jim. You know he did something like this before, don't you?'

I sighed. Like many inner city churches, mine has in its congregation a fair number of disturbed and inadequate people. Jim came to church on and off, and apparently had done so over many years, when he was not in prison. He once confessed to me that he had stabbed a man in some fight over a woman. I think it was the only woman he had ever loved. Jim had not been in church recently, but I had seen him hovering outside the church once or twice in recent weeks as if trying to make up his mind whether to come in. Once I had crossed the road to go and speak to him, but he had instantly scurried away.

'Do you have any reason for saying this, Sid? You haven't talked to him recently?'

'Haven't seen him for months.' Sidney stared at the floor uncomfortably.

'Then why do you think . . . ?'

'It's just a feeling. He might have done something like this.'

I had a prickling feeling of alarm, a realisation that this event might cause much trouble among the members of our congregation. I said, in a quiet but firm voice, 'Sidney, it's for the police to find out who the attacker was and why he did it. At this stage, it could have been anyone. We don't even know who the poor man is who was stabbed. You must be very, very careful, if you talk to the police, not to indulge in wild accusations.'

'You mean you don't think I should tell them?'

'Not unless you have any proper evidence, no.'

I was suddenly afraid for Jim. If Sidney mentioned him, the police might be after him, and find him guilty of other, minor crimes. They might even arrest him, and who knew what Jim might do then?

Sidney suddenly said, 'Thank you, Richard. I'll think about what you've said.' I opened the door for him and he walked out, stumbling over one of the children's toys in the hall. I went back into my study, tried to clear my mind. I had Jim's phone number in my book, and for a moment it crossed my mind to give him a call. I dismissed this instantly. Experience had taught me that it was often better not to interfere, but let things take their natural course, and it was obvious that my motives for calling Jim might be suspected.

I turned back to my desk. Everything was laid out ready for me to complete my sermon for Easter Sunday. Of all things I have to write in the church year, this is the most difficult. As my father had once said to me, by Easter Sunday, it's all over. Those who come to church only on the Sunday have missed the whole thing. There's nothing to say but 'Christ is risen, amen.'

Time in my Study

I sat down at the desk and looked at the first page. I had been writing about the nature of the resurrection. I was discussing how, from the beginnings of time, man had needed this image of rebirth. The West Kennet long barrow in Wiltshire was aligned so that when the sun rose on the midwinter solstice a ray of light came in and lit up the inner chamber. We do not know what kind of rites were enacted there, but it is almost certain that they were rites of rebirth. Then there are the resurrection myths in other societies, of Osiris in ancient Egypt, Attis, and Mithras in the Greek and Roman empires. Throughout ancient history we have the same potent myths. We can't know exactly what these ancient people believed, but the myths are so similar that it's hard not to argue that they point to some underlying truth, either about human nature, or about the nature of the world we live in. But these myths all point to the same thing: the intervention of the spiritual in our earthly, bodily life.

I have to confess at this point that I, like many other Anglican clergy, do not believe in the physical resurrection. Thank God for the Bishop of Durham having the courage to say out loud what so many of us think. Reading the New Testament carefully tends to support this view. The Christ who appears after his death, to Mary Magdalene and the disciples, is not the same man who was with them before. He appears and disappears in their midst, strangely and suddenly; he is often not recognised; he has the character of a vision. At the same time, he eats with the disciples and asks Thomas to put his hand in his wounds, to show that he is not a ghost.

Despite this, I believe that the symbolism of resurrection represents a very deep and profound truth. At times, when I feel weak and filled with doubt, I wonder if there is any meaning to it, whether it is just wish fulfilment to escape from the appalling reality of man's mortality. The truth is that from the moment man could look into the future and foresee his own death he was in trouble. Let's be honest, the idea of our own personal death is unthinkable, intolerable. Have we just invented these myths as a way of making life bearable, of enabling ourselves to live?

Yet it was thoughts of the resurrection that prompted my 'conversion', if you can glorify it with that name, in Jerusalem, at the Garden Tomb. I laid down my pen and stared ahead at the photograph above my desk of Harriet outside the tomb. Ten years ago I had visited Jerusalem, with Harriet and Thomas when he was a baby, staying with friends in a small flat in the Armenian quarter. This was before I entered the church and at the time I described myself as agnostic. Wandering the streets, leaning against the same gnarled olive trees under which Jesus must have prayed at Gethsemane, I found myself preoccupied by the questions of who this man really was and what was the foundation of this religion which I had always taken for granted and always struggled against. I trailed Harriet and the baby round from one site to the next, visited the exca-vations of the Essene community at Qumran where the Dead Sea Scrolls were found. Brought up a Catholic, Har-riet didn't like to delve too much into reality, preferred to accept things entirely on faith. She said my search was obsessive.

In the darkness, lying in our hot, un-airconditioned room, I would wake night after night and find myself unable to sleep, puzzling these questions. By the time the muezzin started up at five o'clock I would abandon thoughts of sleep and go out on to the terrace to read my books on Christian history in the cool air and watch the sun rising over the roofs of the old city.

It was at the Garden Tomb that an insight came to me. Outside the old wall of Jerusalem, in the face of a quarry that imagination can draw into the shape of a skull, lies a genuine first-century tomb. Carved out of the rock, it contains space for three bodies and on the roof are carved Christian crosses to show that it was once used as a place of worship or pilgrimage. In front of the tomb is a grooved track which sinks to its lowest point in front of the tomb entrance, and to one side, in the groove, would have stood a huge stone, like a gigantic millstone. It was clear to see how it would be relatively easy for a few men to roll the stone downhill to cover the entrance but almost impossible to heave it uphill again.

Our guide said the tomb was re-excavated in Victorian times. I asked him, half jokingly, if any bones were found in it. The guide looked at me, startled. Perhaps nobody had dared to ask him that question before. We stood in the hot sunlight in that peaceful place and I realised that I profoundly wished him to say 'No.' I wanted there to be a mystery; I wanted to believe.

He said he believed that there were not. Of course this didn't mean anything; the graves could have been looted at some earlier time. I went back to our flat and read the narrative in Mark, the earliest and simplest version without angels or earthquakes, and wondered yet again about the identity of the young man who sat in the tomb. I noted the last words of the original ending of Mark's gospel in which the women ran away and said nothing to anyone because they were afraid.

That had been the moment when I decided I wanted to study theology. I felt there was some mystery here to which I wanted to find the key. This was the moment which set me on the way to becoming ordained as a priest.

When I had stood there in the tomb at Jerusalem it had somehow seemed quite real and simple. Something had happened. But now I am trying to explain, to rationalise it.

I cannot do it. To tell the truth, Easter Sunday has for me a shoddy, empty ring. It seems shallow and out of tune with what has happened, like the person who says cheerfully 'Life must go on' to someone who is recently bereaved. After the glorious tragedy of the passion narrative, the alleluias seem like a false, jolly coda. It could be argued that we need that note of lightness, like the joke that breaks up the solemnity and brings everyone back to life after some grave occasion. But my heart is never in it.

The door opened. Thomas looked round it. 'Do you want a hot cross bun?'

'No thank you, Tommy. I'm trying to work.'

'Is it true a man was murdered in the church?'

'We don't know if he's dead yet, Tommy. Let's hope that he's not.'

'Why did it happen?'

Harriet's voice came from the kitchen. 'Tommy, leave your father alone. I told you . . .'

I got to my feet. Work was impossible. I went into the kitchen and paced up and down in agitation, jingling the coins in my pocket and generally driving Harriet to distraction. After a while I said, 'Harriet, somehow I feel responsible. That man came into my church, perhaps he was seeking something. I know that's silly, unlikely, but I feel that I must . . . I'm going to Bart's to see what has happened to him.'

✝o St Bartholomew's Hospital

I parked the car on a meter in a courtyard somewhere in the maze of streets that wind between the various wings of Bart's. As I got out of the car I shivered. It was unseasonably cold, and a shower of fine snow fell, driving along the pavements like dust.

I asked at the main reception and was sent up to the intensive care ward. A nurse rushed past, clearly too busy to be bothered with me. A policeman was sitting on a chair in the corridor outside, his hat in his hands, bored, waiting. I sat down beside him. For some reason we didn't speak.

I don't know how long I would have sat there, not saying anything. After about twenty minutes a doctor came out through the pale green doors in a white coat, carrying some notes. Something about the manner of his appearance reminded me of the priest who pops out through the gilded doors from behind the iconostasis at the climax of the Russian Orthodox mass. He looked at the policeman, then at me, and motioned us into a room at the side.

It was clearly a doctor's office. There was a computer on the desk, and a bank of filing cabinets against the wall which took up too much room and made it difficult to open the door. Papers were strewn in a muddle all over the desk and there was a stale, half-drunk plastic cup of coffee near the edge.

He sat behind the desk and indicated two chairs in front of us.

'Make yourselves comfortable.'

We sat down.

I explained who I was and the doctor seemed to accept that I had a right to be there. Being a vicar is very useful in this way. He said his name was Hunt and he was senior registrar. He tapped his fingers nervously on the desktop and fidgeted in his chair; then he cleared his throat, flipped through the notes, and began to talk without once looking up at us.

'I'm afraid the man came into us in a very bad condition. He had lost a great deal of blood and suffered a respiratory arrest, but we were not able to say for certain for how long. You understand that there is only a very short period, about two minutes, that the brain can be deprived of oxygen before damage results.'

The policeman nodded.

He referred again to his notes. 'We intubated him, put in venous lines, took him into the operating theatre and carried out an emergency thoracotomy, that is, we opened the chest cavity. There was bleeding from the heart and from the pulmonary artery, which was dealt with, and we then removed part of one of the lobes of the lung. There was no damage to other internal organs so the operation was not unduly complicated. We sewed him up but when we removed the ventilator he did not breathe of his own accord. He is therefore being kept ventilated but unless there is any improvement in his condition, which I think unlikely, I'm afraid that he will not survive.'

The policeman sat and wrote all this in his notebook. He had mean, cramped writing and the act of his recording this so painstakingly and with such detachment irritated me.

The policeman asked, 'What was the cause of the injury?'

'It's a knife wound, undoubtedly. Considerable force must have been used to inflict it.'

I asked him, 'Do we know who he is yet?'

'He wasn't carrying any identification,' said the policeman. 'So far no one has come forward to report anyone missing, but of course, it's early yet.'

The doctor leaned forward. He looked tired, seemed bored with the whole thing and because we weren't relatives didn't seem to feel he had to pretend otherwise. 'I don't think there is anything else I can usefully say. Would you like us to call you in the event of his recovering consciousness?'

I told him that I would. He gathered up the file and got to his feet; it was obvious the interview was over.

I had one last question. 'I noticed,' I said, 'that there were cuts on his hands. I wondered . . .'

And now the doctor actually smiled. 'Yes, I noticed that,' he said. 'It occurred to one of us that this might have been some bizarre kind of sacrificial act, that the assailant might have intended to kill him in this way, you know, inflicting the same wounds as Christ and doing this in a church. After all, it is Good Friday.' He paused, watching me, but I did not react at all. 'But I'm afraid there is a much more mundane explanation. Many people will instinctively put up their arms in front of their faces to deflect a blow. It seems to me that he probably used his hands to try to grab the knife and push it away from him. That would be entirely consistent with the injuries we found.'

The Man Dies

I arrived back home to find Harriet and the children sitting down to eat supper round the kitchen table. As always, on Good Friday, we had fish. Harriet had bought plaice for the children but for us a beautiful sea bream. A candle was lit, and Harriet, who was raised as a Catholic but now says she is agnostic, was wearing black, because she liked to keep up the traditions. Good Friday supper in our house is always spent just with the family and is always a very solemn occasion.

Harriet didn't ask me what had happened and we put Thomas and Joshua to bed. They were quite lively and began to play a silly game with the duvet covers which had us all laughing and fooling around. When they were finally settled a tremendous weariness came over me and I said that I wanted to go to bed. I ran a bath and soaked there, listening to Harriet tidying up in the kitchen downstairs.

The phone rang. Not many people who knew me well would call on Good Friday evening. I strained my ears but I couldn't hear any of the conversation. Then I heard Harriet coming up the stairs. She put her head round the door.

'It was the hospital. The doctor said that the man has died. He was taken off the life support systems about an hour ago. He said that he thought you would want to know, in case you were saying prayers for him tonight.'

I said, 'That was very thoughtful of him.' Frankly, I was surprised that he had thought of this.

'I'm not sure. He might have been ironical.'

'Come and sit here with me.'

Harriet and I have been married for twelve years. Our first baby, a daughter, conceived before we were married, was stillborn, and that was when Harriet had announced that she no longer believed in God. We had suffered terribly together after her death; while such strains can drive some people apart, this tragedy had brought us closer; despite all the differences between us Harriet is my rock and the one on whom I can always count whatever happens. She is slim and lovely at just forty and one of the most generous people I know.

She sat on the loo seat and watched me, fondly.

'Hurry up and get out of the bath,' she said, 'I want to make love to you.'

Her gaze upon me was already arousing. I got out of the bath and stumbled into the bedroom. She didn't take off her clothes and I didn't bother to dry myself; she threw herself on to the bed and I pulled her towards me and we made love fiercely and quickly. For me there was something sharp and almost painful in it, and more intense than usual; a contact with death often makes us cling more tenaciously to life and the pleasures it can bring us. My emotions were aroused and I wanted to share them; perhaps I wanted also to seek a temporary oblivion.

We got into bed and Harriet turned off the light. We lay with our arms round one another and she fell asleep instantly. I lay awake for a long time, watching the lights from the cars passing in the street, casting shadows on the ceiling. For some reason that I couldn't understand, I was afraid.

The Easter Service

On Sunday morning the children were up early opening their Easter eggs. Silver paper was strewn across the living room and there were chocolatey finger-marks on the door. I had been up before dawn for our early service; now I had a break before the main event. Harriet made preparations for lunch, to which some friends and family were coming, and I went across the road to my study in the church to try to put the finishing touches to my Easter sermon.

I looked at the pages in front of me, dully. Once again I was assailed by doubt. Was this really what they wanted, expected of me? Didn't they just want simple words of faith, the traditional story reaffirmed? What was I doing here at all if I didn't believe, if I could talk only vaguely about mysteries and symbolism, trying to justify my own lack of real belief?

I picked up my pen and crossed out a paragraph. There was a knock on the door.

A man in a suit was standing in the doorway. He had a wallet in his hand which he opened up to me, and I recognised him at once as the detective I had complained to at the Stoke Newington Police Station concerning their treatment of Mercy. Perhaps he didn't want to be reminded of this; at any rate he made no mention of our previous meeting.

'Detective Chief Inspector Stone,' he said. 'I would like to have a few words with you. Do you mind if I come in?'

'No, please do.' Although I know it is very rude, and I try never to do this, I couldn't help glancing at my watch.

Detective Chief Inspector Stone sat down opposite me. He was a haggard-looking man, greying slightly; his suit was shabby, with dandruff flecking the collar. He seemed in an irritable mood; perhaps he was annoyed at having his Easter Sunday ruined. He said, 'I hope you don't mind my calling in on you like this, unannounced. If you didn't mind, I thought that I would come to the service, hear what you had to say. Try to get the feel of the place, if you understand.'

I said that he was very welcome, but that I only had about twenty minutes to finish my sermon. I could give him a few minutes, then perhaps he would like to sit and wait in the church.

Stone said, 'A very serious crime has been committed.

So far, we have very little to go on. I hope that I can count on your help.'

'Of course. But I think I told the detective sergeant everything I know yesterday, when I made my formal statement.'

He was looking at me oddly. The way he stared made me quite irritated, in fact more than that, quite angry. I began to worry that Sidney might have said something to him about Jim, and that he expected me to say something about it. Well, if that was the case, he was wasting his time.

'The post-mortem was carried out yesterday,' Stone continued. 'Death was caused by a single blow with a long-bladed knife, entering between the sixth and seventh ribs, piercing the lung, the apex of the heart, and the pulmonary artery. It was twisted before it was pulled out, to cause the maximum damage.' He paused. 'It's not easy to kill someone with a knife, you know.'

I had never thought about this. Again, the tone in Stone's voice and the manner of his questioning made me uneasy.

'I'm sorry, I don't follow you.'

'What I'm saying is that this seems to have been a deliberate, perhaps premeditated, murder. It wasn't a frenzied attack by a madman, or someone trying to protect themselves who happened to have a weapon to hand. No, this was a cold-blooded killing by someone who knew what he was doing.'

'I see.' I was taken aback; I couldn't see what this had to do with me.

'But there's another problem. Somebody is very keen to make sure that we don't get to the bottom of this.' Again he kept his eyes on me, no doubt waiting for my reaction. 'Well, I suppose I had better tell you what's on my mind. The truth is, something quite extraordinary has happened. They telephoned this morning, at about 6.15, to say the body has been stolen from the mortuary.'

The Body Vanishes

After he had said this there was a long silence in the room. The first thing that came into my head was that somebody was playing the most extraordinary kind of practical joke. I wondered if it was Stone, his way of getting back at me for what I had said to him weeks ago over the incident with Mercy. I thought of what Harriet had said, that the doctor on the phone might have been ironical. It actually crossed my mind at that moment that perhaps they were all playing some savage kind of trick on me.

But that was paranoid. A man had died. My thoughts were utterly egocentric. I pushed them to the back of my mind and forced myself to think clearly. Perhaps this kind of thing was not uncommon. Perhaps dozens of bodies were illegally removed from mortuaries each year, though I couldn't imagine why, or who would want them. It was just the timing that made this seem so strange. My skin was prickling with that irrational fear which can overtake you, say, in a cemetery on a dark night. I glanced down at my watch; I had a few minutes left. I looked up at Detective Chief Inspector Stone.

'I'm afraid I don't know what to say. When did it happen?'

'In the early hours of this morning, it seems.'

'But how could they steal a body? From Bart's? Didn't anybody see anything?'

'The post-mortem wasn't done at Bart's. It was done in the city mortuary, by a forensic pathologist. The place is locked up at night but there's no one on guard . . .' He rolled his eyes heavenwards. 'It seems it was a piece of cake.'

I got to my feet; I was aware that time was short, and that somehow, despite this shocking news, I had to get through the service. I said, 'I'm sorry, fascinating as it is, I have to go now. Perhaps we could continue this conversation afterwards.'

'Do you mind if I use your phone?'

I sighed and pushed it over to him. He dialled a number and spoke mainly in monosyllables, while I could hear the faint squeaking of a woman's voice in the earpiece. I made a few unnecessary corrections to my sermon, stood up, leaving Stone still talking, and went to the vestry to prepare myself.

I remember little of the service. The church as always

46

was full and decorated with flowers. At the front of the church stood the little Easter garden with its empty papier mâché tomb, made by the children from the Sunday School. The children came up to collect their Easter eggs with happy, eager faces. I ended my sermon with a reference to that so often misquoted saying of David Jenkins, that whatever else the resurrection was it was not just 'a conjuring trick with bones'. We had to understand it in the spiritual sense and not just the physical one. The sermon seemed to go down well; one or two people said that they had particularly enjoyed it, and certainly nobody took me to task about it afterwards.

When I got back to the vicarage Harriet and her sister Frances had the lunch well organised, the children were running round the garden with their three cousins, everything seemed under control; there was nothing in particular that I needed to do. There was that strong feeling of anticlimax which always follows the Easter marathon. Normally I would have sat down in the living room and read the papers, but this morning there was no hope of that. It was two hours till lunchtime. I told Harriet that I had to see someone urgently; I made my apologies to Frances, took the car, and drove down to the city.

The city mortuary is situated near the Barbican, in that no-man's land of huge modern office blocks and streets devoid of life. It is a grey modern concrete building, with the mortuary on the ground floor and the coroner's court and office above it, and from the signs I could see that the building contained, among other things, a family planning clinic. I recognised it only from the presence of police cars outside. There is no large sign saying where the mortuary is. People are not supposed to die; all signs of death are carefully hidden away. Probably if they put up a sign people would complain about it, think it in poor taste; nobody likes to be reminded of their mortality. There were two or three police cars in the street, and police standing about, looking, I must say, fairly bewildered. I went up to one of them and explained who I was, and asked what had happened.

It appears that what had happened was this.

On Saturday morning the body had been transferred here from the hospital, so that the post mortem could be carried out by a forensic pathologist. This had been done early on Saturday afternoon, and the body then returned to one of the storage cabinets. Although there is someone present during the day, the building is not manned at night.

Whoever it was had got in through the ambulance bay at the back. The alarm had gone off, but at that time, in the early hours of Easter Sunday morning, no one had been there to notice. The bell could have rung for hours without anyone hearing it. Just after dawn a police car patrolling the empty streets had heard the bell and driven to the scene. They found the green concertina doors drawn back, but no signs of anything damaged or broken.

The police had informed the mortuary superintendent, who had come down to have a look, and established that one of the bodies, marked as U/K369, was no longer there.

'Was it easy to break in?'

'Child's play. There's just a simple mortice lock, and a

gap between the two doors – easy to force open. Once inside, they could get the keys, no problem . . . Are you waiting for somebody?'

I asked if Detective Chief Inspector Stone was there.

'He's inside. Do you want to wait in here? You can sit down if you like.'

I followed him into the porter's office. There was a tray with a kettle and cheap mugs. I could see the little key cupboard, which hung open, displaying a row of keys hanging on hooks. There was a rather outmoded alarm system mounted on the wall. The policeman sat on the desk.

'This is all a bit of a puzzle, isn't it? What do you make of it?'

'So the lock was forced?' I asked.

'Seems like it.'

'Did they have to break anything else?'

'No. When the porter closed up last night he forgot to lock the key cupboard . . . they could have helped themselves. Besides, the cold storage cabinets there aren't locked . . . they just had to whip the body out and take off with it.'

'But there must be some security . . . don't they have video cameras or anything?'

The policeman laughed. 'Well, I have to say this sort of thing doesn't go on very often, you know. Of course, there's very strict security in all the usual procedures . . . you can imagine what kind of a fuss relatives would kick up if a body went astray. But if someone is determined to take a body . . . well.' The policeman shrugged. 'Is it the

Detective Chief Inspector you're wanting to see?'

I said that it was.

'Hang on a minute. Wait, come down with me. I'll see if he's free.'

We walked down a long corridor. We walked past the post-mortem room and I looked through the glass panels in the door, at the cold comfortless metal tables where the bodies would be laid and the reflections on the shiny white tiled surfaces. We went through into the room where the bodies were stored. There was one large cabinet, with glass panels on the doors. Inside one I could dimly see a body, shrouded in white, spookily reminiscent of the drawings I had seen of Christ bound in grave-clothes in the tomb.

Detective Chief Inspector Stone was in the room. He looked exasperated when he saw me.

'So you've come to see the evidence of the resurrection,' he said to me drily.

I told him I thought the remark in very poor taste.

'Well, what is it then?'

'I wanted to talk to you,' I said. 'I've remembered something that could be important.'

'Yes?' His manner showed me plainly that he had no time for me.

I said, 'I'd rather talk in private, if you don't mind.'

Stone took me across the street to his car. We went and sat in the front seats; I don't know why he chose this place, perhaps it was the only way he could get away from everyone. As I walked with him my heart was pounding. I had nothing to say to him; I didn't know why I was doing this. My mind was racing, trying to think of something rational I could say which would justify my intrusion into his time. I wanted to speak to him, I wanted to find out something which would explain what was happening, but I had no specific detail to impart.

We sat in the car and he lit a cigarette. He looked at me sideways with his shifty eyes. 'Well?' he asked.

I wildly said the first thing that came into my head. 'I thought when I looked at that man in the church that I had seen his face somewhere before,' I said. 'I've just realised what it was. When I was giving my sermon this morning, I was looking at the picture of the baptism of Christ which is at the back of the church, behind the font. The likeness is quite amazing.'

Detective Chief Inspector Stone stared at me. I realised with a cold shock even as I said these words that they were quite true. I must have noticed this, as I had said, during the service, and repressed it, because the thought was so frightening. I began to wonder whether I really had gone mad.

'You can verify it yourself, if you want to,' I said. 'You must have taken photographs of the body in the mortuary.'

'Yes, we have,' said Stone. 'Photographs, dental impressions, fingerprints. There was no identification on the body. Nobody has come forward. We haven't had a lot to go on. Nobody has seen anything, there was nobody answering his description in the local pubs, nothing from the house-to-house calls, nothing from anybody on the street. Nobody has seen a thing, not a dicky-bird. All indoors, having lunch, watching television. They might as well all be dead.'

He looked at me again, inhaled deeply on his cigarette. 'Of course, this theft may make things easier. It's no longer an ordinary assault. Somebody wants to make sure we don't get at the body. Why?'

I said, 'There are some religions who are opposed to post-mortems. The orthodox Jews, I believe, don't like the body being disfigured because they believe this will make things a bit tricky on the day of judgement. Might that be a motive?'

'If it was they were too late. They did the post mortem yesterday.' Stone opened the car door, dropped his cigarette stub and put his foot out to grind it into the tarmac. He slammed the door shut again and turned to face me. 'If you're having any thoughts in that direction yourself, I mean about a body coming back to life, I think you should address yourself to what happens at the post mortem. The body is opened from the throat down to the navel or lower.' He made a graphic gesture with his finger. 'All the internal organs are removed and weighed. The stomach is examined, as are the vital organs. These parts are simply put into a plastic bag and deposited back into the abdominal cavity, which is padded out with wadding before it's all stitched up. If you think that can come back to life again, you've got to be joking.'

'I have no thoughts in that direction, I can assure you,' I said quietly, defensively.

Detective Chief Inspector Stone looked at me coldly.

'There's something I want to ask you, while you're here,' he said. 'In the creed, when you get to that bit at the end, that you believe in the resurrection of the body and the life everlasting – is that meant to refer to Christ's body, or all our bodies?'

I was amazed that he should ask me such a question. I said, 'It refers in fact to everyone's body.'

'So we're supposed to believe this, are we? That our bodies come out of the grave and all that. How can anybody take that rubbish seriously?'

There was no point in trying to enlarge upon it now, or getting into a discussion about all these issues, such as whether Christians really believe in hell, or whether hell is merely absence from God, or how a good God could torment people eternally. I simply let my hands fall in a gesture of passive resignation. Stone got out of the car and I followed him back to the mortuary. When we reached the door he left me without a backward glance and went inside.

I was struck once again by his coldness and rudeness. Couldn't they train the police in communication skills? Or was it just me he disliked for some reason?

I stood in the street, not knowing what to do. The thing was incredible. Of course, there might be reasons for stealing a body. If you take a body before it is identified, you are removing the biggest clue for those who are investigating, because if you don't know who's been murdered it's rather difficult to work out who would have killed him and why. Perhaps they didn't realise the post-mortem would be done so promptly; perhaps they imagined nothing would be done over the bank holiday weekend. It crossed my mind that it might be some medical students playing a macabre practical joke, but this didn't seem to make sense; surely they would have had to come forward and admit to it, the consequences of not doing so would be too awful. Besides, what would they do with the body?

Mary Magdalene's anguished words, fresh from Friday's reading, went through my head: 'They have taken away my Lord, and I know not where they have laid Him.'

✝he Encounter with Jim

The following morning, Easter Monday, when I went out to the shops to buy a paper, I unexpectedly bumped into Jim.

He was standing at the corner of London Fields, smoking a cigarette. He was unshaven and dishevelled and I felt that there was something rather furtive about the look that he gave me.

He turned away, glancing at me out of the corner of his eye, and gave a little wave, the sort of wave you give when you hope somebody will not stop, but just go on their way. I was about to do this, starting to cross the road, when something made me change my mind and go on up to him.

'We haven't seen you for a long time, Jim,' I said cheerily.

'I'm sorry,' he mumbled, 'been rather busy.'

I couldn't think of any word less appropriate to Jim's daily life than this.

'No need to apologise,' I said. 'Do come along one Sunday if you have time.'

'Thanks, Richard, but I don't think I'll come. You see, I've been thinking about it all, and I've decided . . . it's all superstition, all this religious stuff, just like not walking under ladders. I've been walking under a lot of ladders recently, and I haven't had a single pot of paint fall on me yet!' And he began to laugh loudly at his own joke.

Something about the way he laughed gave me an unpleasant feeling. I felt strongly that no purpose would be served in continuing the conversation, and wanted to get away at once. At the same time, I felt a responsibility towards him, that I shouldn't just brush him aside, especially if he was in some kind of difficulty.

'Well, Jim, if you change your mind, you're always welcome, you know that. We'd all like to see you.'

I smiled and turned away, but Jim started to walk along beside me. He walked with a slight limp, and now I could detect a faint whiff of whisky on his breath.

'I've been hearing things,' he said suddenly.

'Hearing things?' I echoed stupidly.

'That somebody was murdered in the church.'

'There was a very unfortunate incident, yes.'

'Do they know who done it?'

'No, Jim, I don't think they do.' I was deliberately keeping my voice cheery, almost flippant, as a way of protecting myself from the very bad vibes I was definitely picking up from him. 'Do you have any ideas?'

'Me? Me? Why should I have any ideas?' His voice had suddenly become slightly menacing. 'Why're you asking me?'

'Oh, just because I see you around quite a bit,' I said. 'I thought if you had been around on Good Friday, you might have seen if somebody odd was hanging about near the church.'

'I was in bed,' he said, suddenly standing still and staring at the ground. 'Was terrible ill, Good Friday, I was. Had to phone the doctor, but he wouldn't come out. Never do these days, you know.'

'Still, I'm glad to see you're better today, Jim,' I said. 'Well, I must be off. Nice to talk to you.'

I crossed the road, towards my house. I could feel his eyes boring unpleasantly into my back as I went. Of course, I couldn't help thinking of Sidney's suspicions, and I suppose it did cross my mind that Jim might be up to no good. But I had no desire to try to find out, to play the amateur detective. Extraordinary though these events had been, I was absolutely sure in my own mind that there was a rational explanation, and that the police would probably in due course dig it out.

✝he Young Journalist

I suppose it should not have surprised me when later that day I had a telephone call from a local journalist, Kevin Brown of the Hackney Gazette. Somebody had given him the tip-off that a man had been murdered at the church and he wanted to talk to me about it.

At first I was very hesitant and circumspect, especially when he raised the issue of the theft of the body. We chatted for a few minutes, and I told him as simply as I could what had happened on the Friday. He asked me whether it was possible for a photographer to come and take pictures of the church, and I said that we had some excellent black-and-white photographs taken over the course of a year by a local photographer who was recording the life of the church, and that he was welcome to come and have a look at these.

He turned up the next day at my office and I gave him a selection of photographs which I had looked out for him. He asked if he could see the church and I took him through. It was a dim, dark day and in the late afternoon twilight the empty church seemed gloomy and sepulchral.

He meandered round, seemingly not very interested, and then we returned to my study.

'So what do you think the meaning of it all is?' he said, looking at me, his pen poised above his thick reporter's notebook. He was a young man, in his twenties, with a checked jacket and slicked-back hair. His impatience and his eagerness betrayed his ambition.

'I don't think there is a meaning. It's a terrible tragedy that this has happened. As to why the body was stolen, I don't have a clue. Have the police offered any theories?'

'They think it might be a Kurdish/Turkish vendetta. The two communities rub along all right some of the time, then something happens, or they just get bored and start provoking one another. Somebody else was knifed locally just the other week; they're working on the theory that it might be a revenge killing.'

'And the theft of the body?'

He shrugged. 'Removing the evidence? Causing grief to the family concerned?'

'There seems to be a distinct absence of grieving relatives.'

He looked up at me sharply. 'So you don't think it was anything supernatural.'

I tried to laugh, but I think it came out rather falsely. 'No, of course not.'

'But it's rather curious, isn't it? I mean, two thousand years ago the disciples turned up at the tomb, found the body gone, and told everyone it had been resurrected. Why didn't they believe that it had been stolen then?'

'Well, of course, this was said by some people at the time. In Matthew . . . chapter twenty-eight, verses eleven to fifteen, let me see . . .' I flicked through the pages of my pocket Bible. 'Some of the watch went to the chief priests, and "they gave large sums of money unto the soldiers, saying, Say ye, His disciples came by night, and stole him away while we slept." But the disciples believed otherwise, because, according to John at least, he had predicted that he would rise again on the third day.'

'So you don't think the same thing could happen these days? I mean, if God made miracles happen two thousand years ago, why shouldn't he do so today?'

His tone annoyed me. 'No, I think that's wrong. If Christ came again today, the story would have to be told rather differently.'

The young man was scribbling in his notebook. 'In what way, differently?'

I tried patiently to explain. 'Well, in those days, people believed in miracles. So, in order to show that Jesus was Christ, the evangelists had to tell stories about the virgin birth, the resurrection, and so on, to demonstrate to people that he was no ordinary man. The problem is that nowadays, miracles are to most people not an aid but an obstacle to belief.'

Kevin Brown looked puzzled. 'Let me get this straight. Are you saying that you don't believe in the virgin birth or the resurrection?'

I knew that, speaking to a journalist, I had to be very careful. It would clearly be unwise just to say 'yes' to such a question. I reflected for a moment, trying to choose my words with caution. 'Well, as you probably know, the Anglican Church is a broad Church. There are basically three main groups within it: the evangelicals, who take the Bible as their starting point and tend to take things more literally; the traditionalists, who think we should keep things much as they are and tend to adhere to the existing doctrine; and then there are the liberals, who on the whole believe in change, in reinterpreting Christianity to make it more relevant to our age. Then of course there are also the radicals – the ones who, one might say, don't believe in God as an external being at all.'

'Like that vicar who was kicked out recently.'

'Exactly.'

'And where do you stand?'

'I'm a liberal.'

'I see.' He jotted this down. 'So, let's be quite clear . . . what do you actually believe?'

I had my answer off pat. 'I believe that the virgin birth and the resurrection didn't happen in actual fact, but that they have an important symbolic meaning. They are important because of what they reveal about ourselves and our relationship to God, and about the nature of God, revealed in Jesus Christ.'

He took this down, jumped up, and thrust his note-book into his pocket.

Harriet was watching as I showed him out.

'What did he want?' she asked me.

'Just to know what I thought of these events, that's all.'

'What did you tell him?'

'Nothing, really.' Harriet didn't press me; she went into the kitchen. But now the journalist had gone, I couldn't help feeling uncomfortable, and that perhaps, in my desire to explain, I had said more than was really wise.

The Gardener

It was on Tuesday afternoon that Mary came to see me in my study, looking breathless and anxious. She is normally very neatly dressed and organised and there was something about her distracted appearance which instantly alarmed me.

'Mary, what is it?' I asked. 'Has something happened?'

'I hope you won't think I'm going mad,' she said. 'I wondered whether I should come and see you at all. Perhaps there's a reasonable explanation for it. It could be his brother or something.'

'Mary, sit down calmly, and let's talk about it. Do you want to say a prayer first, quietly, with me?'

Mary calmed herself, folded her hands across her lap,

and sat very still while I said a short prayer. Immediately she seemed much less agitated. She began to tell me her story. She was one of those people who has to start at the beginning and tell the story at her own pace, so I didn't try to interrupt her; usually I found that just prolonged things.

'Well, I'd gone up to visit my friend Rachel in Stoke Newington, and it was such a lovely day, after all this awful weather we've been having, so I thought I would just go and have a stroll in the park. I like to go to that cafe, you know, in the old house there, and I sat and had a coffee. I saw the man in the garden, he was there for a while, pruning the roses. I just sort of watched him, casually, for some time, while I finished my coffee.'

She paused for a moment and fiddled with the clasp on her handbag.

'When I left I walked past him. I was right next to him, as far away as I am from you. He was just on the other side of the rose bushes, with the clippers in his hand, and he looked up at me as I went past. A terrible shock to me it was, because I could see at once that it was that man in the church. I thought, my goodness, he must have recovered quickly, and then I remembered that you had told me he was dead. He smiled and said, "Hello," and I said, "Hello," back, you know, like you do, and then he said, "Don't you remember me?" I tell you, I was so frightened that I just turned and ran away and I didn't know who to tell so I just came straight here to see you.'

I didn't know what to think. Well, what would anyone have thought? I was silent, considering my response carefully. 'Have you told anyone else about this, Mary?'

'No.' She looked at me, puzzled. 'Should I?'

'No, I don't think so,' I said. 'I think it would be better to keep it to yourself.'

'Do you believe me, Richard? You don't think I'm off my head?'

'Well, you could be right. Perhaps it could be a brother of this man.' I thought for a moment, and then said, thinking aloud, 'But then it would be very odd that he hadn't informed the police about it.'

Mary now seemed worried about this hypothetical brother. 'He might not know. How would he know? Suppose he only saw his brother occasionally? There was no name in the papers. Do you think we should tell the police?'

Again, I gave this very careful consideration. 'Well, it might be an idea to tell the police. This gardener must be employed by the council. I suppose it would be something for them to follow up. But don't be frightened about it, Mary. There'll be a reasonable explanation, don't you worry. Surely you don't believe in ghosts, do you?'

Mary got to her feet. She said, 'Oh, I'm sorry, Richard. I was just being silly, wasn't I? Thank you, you've made me feel much better about it.' She looked at her feet. 'But you will ring the police for me, won't you? I don't like to have anything to do with the police; they'll find some way to blame something on me, like they did with Mercy, you can be sure of that.'

I stood up and opened the door for her. When she had gone I turned and shut the door firmly behind me and stared at the phone. Perhaps I should call the police, but the thought gave me no joy. I could imagine the sardonic voice of Detective Chief Inspector Stone as I tried to explain things. No, I would have to be sure first. Perhaps it was all in Mary's imagination. I looked at my watch. I had an hour before I had to go to a meeting at the church school. I put the answerphone on, locked up my desk and drove up to Clissold Park.

It was a warm, spring-like day. People were relishing the sudden change in the weather, had gone out with their children, feeding the ducks; nannies with pushchairs strolled along in the bright sunlight. I came to the rose garden near the café and stood on the path. It was deserted. In the distance the high war-cry of children's voices came to me from the playground behind the wall.

I stood there for five or ten minutes, breathing in the warm air, looking at the new green shoots on the rose stems. You could see that they had indeed been recently pruned; the stems were green and here and there was a cutting which had fallen to the ground. But now there was no sign of any gardener. I turned and walked back down the path to the road, looking thoughtfully at the ground.

As I reached the gate a man passed me. I glanced up and saw his face. He was wearing bulky gardener's gloves and carried a pair of secateurs, and he looked nothing like the man from the church.

I felt angry and foolish and curiously disappointed. I went to the car and drove back to the school, determined to blot the whole thing from my mind.

The Police Arrest Jim

It was nearly midnight that evening when I received a phone call from the police station to say that Jim Jeffries was there helping them with their enquiries, and that he had specifically asked them to telephone me and let me know.

I was puzzled and taken aback. I groped around in the dark for the flex to the bedside lamp and finally managed to switch it on. Harriet too was awake, wide-eyed and staring at me. 'Does he want me to come up there?' I said.

'No, sir, I don't think there would be any point. You wouldn't be able to talk to him.'

'Is he under arrest?'

'Yes.'

'This isn't to do with the murder, is it?'

'I'm afraid I'm not able to give you that information.'

I tried to think rapidly. I suppose I was angry and confused at having been woken up so abruptly. 'Please let me speak to Detective Chief Inspector Stone.'

'I'm sorry, sir, I was just passing on a message. Detective Chief Inspector Stone is not available.'

I hung up. I turned to Harriet and said, 'They've arrested Jim.'

'Why?' She sat up, running a hand through her tangled hair, and reached for the glass of water by the bed.

'Perhaps they haven't found anyone else to arrest. They've got to be seen to be doing something.' I was also, of course, thinking of Sidney. He couldn't have been stupid enough to inform the police, could he? And I didn't think he had any particular reason to cause trouble for Jim.

I couldn't go back to sleep; neither could Harriet. We lay in the darkness, tossing and turning. She lay close to me and after a while I started to stroke her back and then her thighs; she caressed me in return, also wanting to make love. There was a particular tenderness between us that night, as if she sensed my anxiety and wanted to comfort me and I, too, wanted to reassure her. Finally satisfied by one another, we fell asleep in the early hours, Harriet lying curled up in my arms.

In the morning at breakfast time I rang the police station and was told that Jim had been released just twenty minutes before. He must have come straight to us, because as soon as I had put the phone down the doorbell rang. Harriet let him in, and we went into the study. The children were running round, making a terrible noise, and Harriet was screaming at them because their breakfast was going cold.

Jim looked terrible. His face looked grey with lack of sleep and his clothes were filthy. He had an ugly bruise just under his left eye.

'The police did this,' he said, pointing to it. 'I want to know what's going on. Who put them on to me? Somebody in the church put them on to me. Who was it?'

I was shocked at his appearance, but I wanted to hear the whole story first. I said, 'Please, Jim, sit down.'

'Who was it?' He was insistent.

'I can't answer that question, Jim.'

'Why?'

'Jim, calm down, and let's talk about this. If you haven't done anything wrong, you haven't got anything to be afraid of.'

I regretted saying this at once. In the first place, we know only too well that many innocent people go to jail because the police feel they must make a case against someone. Second, it was all too likely that Jim had not been going straight, and that while I didn't believe that he was capable of murder, he might have been up to other things that were no good.

He waved his finger in the air. 'If I find out who it was I'll kill him.'

'Well, that's why I can't tell you, Jim.'

'Was it you?' He leaned forward suddenly, threateningly. I shook my head.

'Why don't you sit down and tell me what has happened.'

He finally sat down in the old armchair. He told me that the police had twice been to talk to him about his movements on the morning of Good Friday. He had told them he was in bed at home and that he'd had a touch of flu. But when they had checked with his landlady, she had told them that she had definitely heard him going out, and that she remembered this because she was surprised he would go out so early on a bank holiday. They had searched his room, and found that there was no bread knife, in fact, no sharp knife at all.

'I told them I always ate sliced bread and I never bought a joint of meat, but they kept going on and on about it. I told them it wasn't any of their business. Then they asked me why I was lying to them. I said OK, I had gone out, and that I had gone for a walk in the park, and that there weren't any witnesses, and that's why I didn't want to tell them because I knew they were trying to pin this murder on me.

'Well, then they said they wanted me to come in and talk to them and I said, no way. They went on for hours like this and finally they said they were arresting me. I know better than to start a fight with them, that's just playing into their hands, so I went with them. One of them just hit me here, for no reason, just as I was getting into the car.'

I said nothing. It was more than likely that Jim had resisted or provoked them, but I didn't want to suggest this, having no proof, and knowing what had happened to

Mercy. Jim stood up, went over to the window and stared out. He thrust his hands deep into his pockets, as if he were afraid that in his anger he would be unable to control them.

'I really wasn't up to anything, Richard, I swear to you. Can't a man just walk round by himself thinking without being arrested? I was thinking about if I should come to church or not. I wanted to come. It's warm, and there's company. But I didn't feel I should come if I didn't believe in it all. What do you think, Richard?'

I said softly, 'I think you should have come.' I was stricken with the realisation that Jim, in his way, was more honest than I was. He felt he had to believe certain things before coming to take communion, while I consecrated the bread and wine without even knowing deep down what I thought I was doing. How could I tell him what was in my heart?

He turned and looked at me. His eyes were very sad, and suddenly he wasn't angry any more. He said, in a quiet voice, 'Anyway, they haven't got anything on me. They can't prove a thing, can they? They had to let me go. You'll back me up, won't you, if it comes to anything? You'll give me a good reference.'

'Yes, of course I will.'

'Thanks for listening.'

I showed him to the door.

The Painting in the Church

When I crossed the road to the church later that morning to get ready for our Wednesday service, I noticed a police car across the road. My step quickened, expecting some news, but no one was waiting by the door to my office. I checked in the playgroup hall, but the mothers told me that no one had been asking for me. I unlocked the door between my office and the main church and there, at the back of the hall, standing in front of the painting of the baptism, was Detective Chief Inspector Stone.

I crossed the gleaming polished floor and went to stand beside him.

Stone looked straight ahead, not acknowledging my presence at first. Then he asked, 'Who did this painting?'

'A man called Durfield.'

'Did he do the frescoes?' He waved his arm at the pictures on the wall.

'They're not frescoes. They were actually painted on canvas and fixed to the wall. Yes, he did them all.'

'I have to say you were right. The resemblance is quite remarkable.' He took from his pocket a photograph of the corpse. The face had that odd, disembodied look which even in a photograph tells you that the person is dead. This is the greatest argument in favour of the soul that I can think of. When people are alive, even if they are gravely ill and in a coma, there is still something in their faces, some tension, some spark. Probably a doctor could explain it to me, could give a reason, something to do with rigor mortis or the configuration of the muscles, I don't know, but a dead person is undoubtedly and unmistakably dead, even in a photograph.

When they let me view my mother's dead body, at the age of six, I said at once, 'But where has she gone?' As a child I could see immediately that she was no longer there. I have felt the same thing, again and again, when I have gone to look at a dead person. Now I stared at the photo of the man with fascination.

'We are doing an artist's impression for the papers,' said Stone. 'I thought I might ask the artist chappie to come up and have a look at this.'

I said I had no objection.

'This man, Durfield,' said Stone. 'Did he use a live model?'

'I believe he might have done.'

'Could I speak to him? Just on the rare off-chance, you know, we have to follow up every angle, that he might have been related to the deceased.'

I had a sudden intuition, then, that this business had also got to Chief Inspector Stone. I could see that he didn't know which way to turn, that his investigation was getting nowhere, and that he was seeking a rational explanation for all this as desperately as I was.

'I can look for his number. I must have a record of it somewhere. I believe he was living in Suffolk. He must be quite an age by now; I do hope that he hasn't died, but I'm sure I would know of that.'

He followed me into my office and I went through the drawers of my desk. I found the address and telephone number and gave it to Stone. Then I said, 'Perhaps it would be better if I spoke to him. It might be difficult for him, talking to the police.'

Stone nodded. I dialled the number myself. I was lucky, he was in; a rich, frail voice answered me.

'Is that James Durfield?'

He confirmed that it was.

'This is Richard Page, the vicar at London Fields . . . you remember? I wanted to ask you . . . the model of the painting of the baptism of Christ. Was it a real model that you used?'

He said that it was painted from his head. It was, as he remembered, modelled on the head of Christ in Piero della Francesca's 'Resurrection' which is in the National Gallery.

It is curious how, in all ages and in every different style

of sculpture or painting, the face of Christ is instantly recognisable. It is something to do with the thin, elongated face, the long, straight, high-ridged nose, the heavy eyes, the sensual mouth. Add to this long hair and a beard and the image is complete; so familiar that we feel that if we saw him we would recognise him in the street.

I thanked Durfield very much, told him how much the pictures meant to me, asked him, as an afterthought, if he would mind writing about them for the parish magazine.

I hung up and looked at Stone.

'Did you hear that?'

'No.'

'It was from a painting in the National Gallery.' I wrote the artist and title down on a piece of paper and handed it to him. 'Perhaps you could go and study that next.'

He made an angry sound in his throat, almost like a dog growling, and then turned abruptly on his heel, and left the room.

The Article Appears

To my relief the article in the *Hackney Gazette* on Thursday outlined the story of the murder and the missing body, but very little of my interview with the young journalist. In fact he had reported my words rather accurately. I spread the newspaper out across the desk in my office at the church. There was an artist's impression of the dead man, but I didn't think it was a good likeness. The police were urging anyone who knew or had seen this man to step forward.

Over the last few days, several members of the church had come up to me and asked what I thought about these strange events. Most of them said it lightly, laughing, almost making a joke of it, but I could see that underneath many were perturbed. Mary, clearly, hadn't kept what she had seen to herself. One or two people asked me if I thought Mary was all right, because she was sure that what had happened meant some special sign had been sent to her, or to the church. Tessa told me that she told the women's prayer group all about it at their meeting on Wednesday.

Tessa stood in front of me now, peering at the paper. She was in a hurry, her hair was disarrayed, and her trousers bulged oddly because she hadn't taken off her bicycle clips. She said that she was a little anxious about all this. People in the church were taking different sides and wanted to know more clearly what I believed, she said. Liberalism was all very well, but I was aware, like her, that there were many people in the church who did have a more simple and more literal faith. I was always careful in my sermons not to advocate too strongly one view or the other, because I knew that my church was particularly mixed, containing recent immigrants, black people who had been born and raised here, poor white East Enders and well-to-do professionals and intellectuals. When speaking, I always tried to find the points of agreement and not to cause too much controversy. I knew that I was forever in danger of alienating one group in satisfying another.

No one had ever taken me to task about my sermons, and I often wondered whether that was because no one really concentrated on them. As long as I had a good beginning and a safe conclusion, the likelihood was that not too many listened to what went on in between. But perhaps, if the congregation were looking to me for some leadership, maybe to quell their understandable fears that something supernatural was going on, it was time for me to speak out clearly. Certainly I would give it some thought.

I looked up at Tessa, who was hovering near the door. 'Perhaps I should say something,' I said. 'If not in a sermon, then possibly in the parish magazine.'

She turned back towards me, urging me in her quiet way. 'I think it would be a good idea.'

'Are you in a terrible hurry? You don't want to have a cup of tea?'

Tessa glanced at the door, then at her watch, and then smiled. 'All right,' she said, 'but I'll just have to lock up my bicycle.'

While she went outside I boiled the kettle and poured the tea. Tessa came back and sat on the edge of the armchair.

'What did Mary say at the prayer group?' I asked her.

Tessa said, 'She felt that God was sending her a special message. She said that whatever anyone else said, she knew when she saw this man's face that it was the face of our saviour. She said that she was a little hurt that you didn't really believe her.' Tessa paused, looking at her hands. 'She said that you thought it might have been the man's brother.'

Then, as I sat with the warm mug of tea in my hands, I realised that something very odd had happened. It hadn't occurred to me at all that Mary might have had some kind of vision. Instead, I had taken it as a statement of absolute reality that Mary had seen a man who looked like the dead man. I felt myself going hot all over with a kind of embarrassment.

'What's the matter, Richard?'

I sipped my tea. 'Oh, I was just thinking that I hadn't handled Mary very well, that's all. I must think about it, and have a talk with her.'

Tessa got up from her chair, put the empty mug down on the tray, and came over to me. She put her hand on my arm and squeezed it gently. 'Oh, I'm sure you handled her much better than I did,' she said. 'But do write that article. Do you promise?'

'I promise.'

She took her hand off my arm, and hovered in the room for a moment. The faint aura of some perfume hung about her, and I was reminded for a moment of Harriet. I looked up at Tessa and smiled. Then she suddenly said, 'I must go,' backing away from me and nearly colliding with the coffee table. She was gone in an instant, leaving me to my thoughts, and for some reason which I couldn't under-stand I felt abominably uncomfortable.

The Incident in the Rose Garden

On Saturday it was fine so Harriet and I had the afternoon off and took the children to Clissold Park to ride their bicycles. As always, when we'd fed the ducks, looked at the peacocks and deer and been to the playground, we went for a cup of tea for us and an ice-cream for the boys at the café.

The children ran off in the sunshine and went to play a game jumping off the wall down into the shrubbery. I glanced over at the rose garden, then turned to Harriet, about to tell her what Mary had said to me the other day.

Harriet was staring very oddly in that direction. I turned and followed her gaze. There was a gardener there, dressed in old clothes and dirty gardening gloves, pulling out the weeds. He was bent over and I couldn't see his face. Harriet turned her head away and went back to drinking her tea without saying anything. Then she excused herself and went off to the loo.

I sat and waited for a few minutes. Then I got up and walked down from the terrace to enter the rose garden. The man was a few feet from me, bending right over. He looked up when I stood there and straightened up, putting his hand in front of his eyes to shield them from the sun.

I didn't say anything. I was incapable of doing so. My throat felt dry, my legs felt numb and my heart began to thump in the most alarming manner. It was the same man. There was no doubt in my mind at all. I turned round and walked away from him at once, running up the steps, looking for Harriet. She wasn't there, and her bag had gone from the chair. Unreasoning terror swept over me; I went round behind the café to the loos but she was not there either. I ran back on to the path; neither the children nor Harriet were in sight. They had vanished.

I felt a panic sweep over me that I had felt only once before, when Thomas had gone missing for twenty minutes in a crowded market on holiday in France. I looked around, began to run. As I hurtled down the path I heard a voice calling me, 'Dad, Dad.' I turned round. Thomas was waving to me. They were all standing further down the path, Thomas, Joshie and Harriet, waiting for me.

We got back to the car. My heart was still pounding and I felt sick. Harriet and I looked at one another but said nothing. It was only later in the evening, when the children were asleep and we were sitting in front of a fire, probably the last we'd light now till the winter, that I asked Harriet if she had seen what I saw in the park.

She didn't look at me at first. She said, 'You mean the gardener.'

'Yes, I mean the gardener.'

She seemed puzzled. She put down the pair of Joshie's trousers she was mending and looked up at me. 'I don't understand. Why are you asking?'

'I saw you staring at him.'

'For some reason he looked familiar, that's all.'

'You didn't think that he looked like the man who died?'

'Richard, what on earth do you mean?' She stared at me, her face showing confusion, almost shock.

'Well, did you?'

'You're not thinking straight. You forget that I never saw him.'

I had indeed forgotten this. It shocked me for a moment, as if I were losing my grip on reality. I said, 'Yes, yes, of course.'

She picked up the trousers and went on sewing. 'Richard, what are you thinking about?' There was a slightly sharp, nervous edge to her voice.

'I'm thinking that first Mary thought that he looked like the dead man, and then me.'

'Why didn't you say anything at the time, in the park?'

'Oh, I didn't want to bring it all up because of the children. I didn't want to put any ideas into their heads. Harriet, you don't think I'm going off my head, do you?'

'Oh, Richard, of course not.' She said this promptly,

but I thought she sounded hesitant and unsure.

I wanted to talk about it, wanted to share my feelings. 'I thought that on Monday I would ring the council and ask about it. Mary saw him as well, you know, last week, and she thought the same thing. She thought perhaps we should tell the police, in case it was a brother or some relative.'

'But the picture has been in the papers. Surely if it was someone they would have come forward.'

'Not everybody reads the papers.'

'But everybody knows somebody who does, don't they? Well, why don't you tell the police? Let them follow it up.'

'Because I don't like the police.' I had to admit, if I was honest, that the deep distrust between me and Detective Inspector Stone was growing. I doubted very much if they would follow up anything I suggested to them. I got up from my chair and went to the window, drew back the curtain and stared at the dark shadow of the church across the street. How would I get the information out of the council? It would be easy for the police, difficult for me. Or I could go and talk to the man directly. Well, why didn't I? There was nothing to stop me.

Harriet's voice was sharp, alarmed almost. 'Richard, what are you looking at?'

I turned back to look at Harriet, let the curtain drop. 'Oh, nothing, nothing.' I was tired; I was becoming overwrought, seeing shadows where there were none. I turned and went across the room, kissed the top of her head. 'Come on,' I said, 'let's go to bed.

✝The Limits of Theology

In fact I did nothing about trying to find out about the gardener. The next few days were very busy, and on top of everything else I had to do, Chris Shaw rang to remind me that he urgently needed my letter for the next issue of the parish magazine, which was otherwise ready to go to the printer. I told him he would have it the next day, and in the evening shut myself up in my study, conscious of my promise to Tessa.

What do I believe? How could it be that I don't know the answer to this simple question? Here I was, an Anglican vicar, and people came to me for answers. Could I not even begin to answer this?

I sat at my typewriter, fidgeting in irritation, forced myself to start. This is the letter that I finally wrote.

Dear friends,

When I was a child I believed in God because my father did. Even after my mother's tragic death his faith did not fail him. I grew up with daily prayers and the promise that God would love, God would forgive, God would make everything all right. But manifestly he did not make everything all right; my mother would never come back. So, as I grew up, my faith gradually altered. I stopped believing that God would answer my prayers in a direct way. Rather than 'God, please let me have a new mother,' my prayers changed to 'God, please help me to not mind about not having a mother.' But I couldn't help noticing that my prayers seemed to have no effect, either outwardly or inwardly, and that around me people continued to suffer and die and God did not seem to do anything about it. Eventually I stopped praying at all.

At the age of about fourteen I announced to my father that I did not believe in God and went through my agnostic phase. I rejected Christianity, but I still took an interest in spiritual and religious matters. As I grew older, I toyed with Buddhism, read about Hinduism and Sufism, and read the works of Jung. I did not really need God at this time; I was quite happy in my work and my relationships and, like many young men, it did not really occur to me that I would ever become old or ill, or die. Whether there was a God or not didn't seem to be of either emotional or practical importance; rather it was a matter for intellectual curiosity.

Then, in my late twenties, when Harriet and I were first married, we went to Jerusalem and I had my conversion experience at the Garden Tomb.

I was determined to find out what Christianity meant. Starting out in a new direction, I began a three-year theology course at King's College. The study of theology proved a gruelling time for me. The Anglican tradition has always given freedom to people to doubt, has even encouraged them, because doubt forces people to think, rather than accept things on blind faith. But now I realise that this process of questioning made it singularly difficult for any sensitive and intelligent person to go through the course without their capacity for faith being altered and, in my case, undermined. I sometimes wondered if it were not the very worst kind of training that a priest could have.

One of the major problems of Christian theology has always been trying to marry the historical figure of Jesus with the Christ of faith. Is Christ God in human form – the Docetic heresy – or is he human but inspired by or adopted by God – the Adoptionist heresy? If he is both fully human and fully divine, the answer which the Council of Chalcedon came up with in AD 451, how are these two opposites combined, and what happens where they seem to be contradictory? For example, Christ died on the cross, but God cannot die, so how can Christ be God?

I had thought that in going back and trying to understand who Jesus was, I would understand more. But we cannot know more than a tiny amount about the historical Jesus, the records do not exist, and it is all too long ago. And even if we did know a great deal more, how much difference would this make? There would still be the problem of interpretation. As soon as we look at Jesus and study him, it becomes clear that he was an itinerant Jewish preacher, who believed that the end of the world was about to come, who rejected the dogma of the Jewish religion, and who preached many things that are contradictory. He does not say that he is God, only refers to himself as the enigmatic 'Son of Man'. I could not see how this fitted in with the Christ, the man without sin, the Son of God, who is one with God, and whose death redeemed our sins.

Studying theology, it becomes clear that all these beliefs about Christ were worked out much later, by men, in an attempt to explain the inexplicable. The early schisms or heresies within the church were the process by which men decided what they should believe. Many beliefs were drawn up to dispel the many heresies which arose in the early centuries of the Church. For example, in our creed we say 'The resurrection of the body' because the early church was countering the influence of the gnostics, who rejected the world of the material as evil, and focused on rebirth of the spirit. We studied the arguments by which the beliefs of the church came into being, the doctrine of the incarnation, the nature of the Trinity. Look at the titles of some of the essays I wrote. Did Jesus foresee his death, and if so, what significance did he attach to it? Was Christ a pre-existent being who became incarnate? What does the gospel evidence tell us about the resurrection of Jesus? Is God omnipotent? Discuss.

How was it possible to examine these questions honestly and still believe?

And as if this isn't enough, we also cannot deny that our beliefs have changed over the ages. When I became ordained as a priest, I had to assent to the thirty-nine articles of faith, as laid out it the 1662 Book of Common Prayer. The thirty-nine articles were agreed at a convocation held in London in the year 1562 'for the avoiding of diversities of opinions'. Technically these form the doctrine of the church, but in practice many of them now seem antiquated and few would be able to believe in them as fact.

Nobody but a handful of extreme fundamentalists now believes in the literal roasting of bodies in hell, in heaven as a physical realm or in the resurrection of our own material bodies after death. Now people talk about hell as 'separation from God' and heaven as being 'united with God', and other such vague concepts. Yet the loss of Satan as a real figure also creates problems in trying to understand why evil exists. And how much sense does it make to accept a non-realist view of Satan, saying he is a personification of the idea of evil, and yet keep a realist view of God? In fact, the loss of Satan seems to have had much the same effect as the collapse of the communist bloc and the end of the cold war – we are left puzzled and confused, not knowing how to act.

So where do I go from there? I certainly do not feel ready to reject religion altogether. There is no doubt that the story of Christ's birth, life and passion still exerts a powerful influence on us. But it works at the emotional, intuitive level, not the rational. I believe that theology has backed itself into a corner. It is impossible to use logical or rational thought to explore the intuitive and emotional truths of myth, symbolism, and mystery. I believe that rational thought can have no place in examining these questions.

So, what do I believe in? I believe in the truth of the myth, the importance of its symbolism.

Therefore I must go on in faith, remaining open to what comes.

Harriet came in just as I was finishing, carrying a mug of coffee. 'The phone kept ringing for you,' she said, 'but I said you were busy and asked them all to call you back in the morning.'

'Thank you.' I took the mug from her gratefully. 'What do you think of this?' I asked her, handing her the type-written sheets.

Harriet read the letter through slowly and carefully. 'Well, I think it's very honest,' she said. 'But are you sure you want to say this? You don't think it's going to upset people?'

'Tessa thought that I should be clear about what I believe . . . people want to know what I think.'

'Tessa isn't always right, you know.'

I thought I detected a trace of sharpness in her voice, but perhaps I imagined this. She handed me back the pages. Harriet's negative reaction didn't particularly alarm me; I was pleased with what I had written, and thought that on the whole it would do more good than harm. 'Anyway, it's too late, I can't write another one,' I said, anxious not to prolong the discussion any further. 'I promised it to Chris in the morning.'

'Well, that's that then,' said Harriet briskly, and left the room.

The Police Call

A couple of days after I had written this letter the detective sergeant from Stoke Newington Police Station rang and asked if he could speak to me on a confidential matter.

I said of course, and made an appointment for later that afternoon. The PCC meeting was starting at 7.30 that evening, and as usual we were holding it in the living room in the vicarage, which was larger than my office and much more warm and comfortable than the church. I suggested he came at seven, if half an hour would be enough.

He said that would be fine, and arrived promptly on time. I offered him the usual cup of tea, which he accepted, and we sat down in my study.

'You know Jim Jeffries,' he said.

I suppose I had been waiting for this. 'Yes, of course,' I said.

'He comes to church regularly?'

'When he's not in prison,' I said.

The sergeant was sharp. 'So you know about that.'

'Of course I know

'Do you know what for?'

'Petty theft, receiving, that kind of thing.'

'Did you know that twenty years ago he did time for causing grievous bodily harm?'

'Twenty years is a long time.'

The sergeant looked at me coldly. 'You take some kind of oath, don't you, you vicars. Of confidentiality. If someone confesses something to you, you won't reveal it to anyone.'

'We don't actually take any specific oath,' I said, 'but I think that is fairly generally understood.'

'Are you protecting him? If he confessed anything, you wouldn't tell us, would you?'

'No, I wouldn't. But in this instance, I can assure you that he's said nothing to me that would be of any use to you.'

'I see.'

He sat for a minute, glancing round the bookshelves. I found my thoughts wandering. This was the kind of issue I had often thought about in the past. There is, of course, a limit to confidentiality. Naturally, if anyone confessed a crime such as sexually abusing their children, there was no way I could sit back and allow the child to go on suffering. Although the Anglican church retains the sacrament of confession, it is seldom used, and there is not the formal confessional of the Catholics. I don't know what they would do in such circumstances, but in my view there are occasions on which not to breach confidentiality would be wrong. Whether I would tell the police if Jim had confessed the murder to me I don't know. I would certainly urge him to give himself up, but I'm not sure that I would betray him to the police if he didn't.

The sergeant brought me back to earth with a bump.

'He wasn't in church on Good Friday.'

'No.'

'Has he been since?'

'No, he hasn't been for a few weeks. I did see him recently, and he told me he was having doubts.'

This seemed to amuse the Detective Sergeant. 'Well, he's not alone there, is he?' he said, getting to his feet. 'I'm sorry for taking up your time.'

As he left I saw that he had in his hand a newly printed copy of the parish magazine.

✝The PCC

There was a funny mood that evening at the PCC. I don't think that I can have imagined it. We discussed a report compiled by the Social Responsibility Committee on 'Black Christians in Stepney' and the policy of St Michael's towards giving to outside charities. We also discussed the use of 'inclusive language' in the Sunday service and decided, as an experiment, to introduce a couple of minor changes into the wording of the service, in order to eliminate one or two instances of male-dominated emphasis in the liturgy. We also discussed the use of incense in church, because one or two people had complained about it last time it was used and in particular an elderly parishioner, Doreen, had said that it brought on her bronchitis.

Tessa was also at the meeting. She too seemed in an odd mood, and was dressed, unusually for her, in an attractive cotton dress. She wore her hair loose, and I caught her smiling at me once or twice as if we shared some secret knowledge. I think she felt that she was on my side against all this pettiness.

At the end of the meeting Mercy came into the kitchen where I was loading the used mugs into the dishwasher. She mentioned my letter in the parish magazine and said that she didn't understand it. She wanted to know whether I had ever had any kind of religious experience.

This was not an easy question to answer when preoccupied with dirty mugs and a dishwasher. Straightening up, I said that I found it hard to define a religious experience. Every time I hear a beautiful piece of music, or see something lovely, or feel close and loving towards someone, or visit a mother with a healthy newborn baby, I am filled with a sense of joy and meaning. I see God, or the miraculous, in all these things. I could not say that I had any separate sense of an experience that I would say was religious apart from these things.

Then Mercy said abruptly, 'I went with Mary up to Clissold Park. Have you been to Clissold Park to see for yourself?'

I must admit that I felt irritated; I felt that everyone was getting at me. I was afraid to admit to her what I had seen and all the implications of it; besides, I was tired. I turned and ushered her out into the hallway. As she put on her coat and hat I told her, 'Perhaps I shall go on Monday.'

'Oh, please do,' she answered, 'And tell me what you find.'

The Scent Goes Cold

I didn't go to Clissold Park. I went as far as the gates, and then turned back. Instead I drove down to the council office responsible for parks and recreation. It is the same office that is responsible for the cemeteries, so I'd had reason to go there before.

I had to think of some story to tell them. I would have to make up some fiction, some excuse as to why I wanted to know who this gardener was. I do try never to lie, but to always tell the truth in everything, except little things when it doesn't matter, 'white' lies, as we call them. So it went against the grain to tell a council official a story which I had completely concocted from start to finish.

I said that I had spoken to the gardener on duty in Clissold Park the Saturday before last, and that he had dropped a pouch, and that I wanted to return it to him.

The woman from the council said that if I wanted to do that I could leave the pouch with her, and she would get it to him.

I said that I didn't have the pouch and that she could ring me if she found out who it was, and I would bring it in to them.

She said I should either hand it in or give it to the police.

I said that I wanted to be sure myself that it was returned to the right man. At this the official became a little irritated. I am sure that if I hadn't been wearing a dog collar she would have thought I was up to no good.

She repeated, very patiently, as if I were quite stupid, that this was the only way she could go about it. I left my number and said I would try to drop the pouch in, but that I was very busy. She said she would pass on the message.

I left the building, stood on the busy street, disoriented. Cars buzzed backwards and forwards in front of my eyes. Lying is clearly a skill that does not come naturally to me; to lie successfully, you clearly need great skills of anticipation and foresight. Still, I was a novice at it. With time no doubt it became easier and easier; I might even become as accomplished as some of the boys in the church school, who lied instinctively, unable to recognise the truth any more.

Three days passed and there was no phone call. Twice I went to Clissold Park, sneaking up there in odd moments between visits to parishioners without telling Harriet, but there was no gardener. I went into the café and asked if the gardener ever came in to buy tea or have a chat but they knew nothing.

On the fourth day I scribbled a note to Detective Chief Inspector Stone, telling him that I had seen a man two Saturdays before at the rose garden in Clissold Park who appeared to be a council-employed gardener, and who seemed to bear a remarkable resemblance to the dead man. I wrote that another parishioner had seen him on a previous day pruning the roses, and also noticed the resemblance. I thought I ought to let him know in case it turned out to be a relative. I posted the letter and waited in anticipation for something to happen. There was no answering phone call. I thought that probably Stone had read it with exasperation and put it in the bin. Perhaps that is where it belonged.

I should at that moment have forgotten the whole incident, and nearly succeeded in doing so; indeed, if I had never sent that note it is quite possible that nothing further would have happened. But something strange had happened to me. I wanted to believe that this bizarre series of events had a meaning. I couldn't bear to think that it hadn't. When nothing more happened, when the trail seemed to go completely cold, I had a feeling of disappointment, that things were out of joint, that I had been somehow cruelly set up and then let down. I felt that if this event could be meaningless, the cruel murder and the theft of the body meaningless and unexplained, then everything could be meaningless and unexplained. In other words, I felt I had lost the ability to live in faith. Everything became colourless, all the things I had previously enjoyed, even my relationship with Harriet and the children.

I was suffering the kind of crisis that is, perhaps, not unusual among the clergy, a spiritual depression, a temporary or not-so-temporary loss of faith. I wrestled with this inside, not knowing what to do to help myself. I was forgetful, miserable, and withdrawn. In the meantime I went about the parish, performing my duties, taking services in the church, attending meetings, visiting the sick, writing letters and preparing the class for confirmation, and depositing my monthly cheque from the church commissioners into my bank account.

The Detective Chief Inspector Accuses

Monday is my day off. There was no reason why Detective Chief Inspector Stone should know this. The children were at school, and Harriet was out teaching, as she was three days a week. The house was in silence and I was lying on my back on the living-room floor, staring at the ceiling, and listening to a Bach cantata on Classic FM.

There was a knock on the door. It was the same kind of loud, peremptory knock that bailiffs give. I had been in many houses of the parish where people live in daily fear of the bailiffs. Once I was there with a woman when they called because she hadn't paid her poll tax or her council tax. When she refused to open the door they had pushed a form through the letterbox for her to fill in saying what they could take. She had written angrily, her fingers pressing hard on the pencil: 'Two children under five, one ageing husband, one cracked loo seat, a broken chair.' Then she had passed it out again.

I tightened my dressing-gown cord and went to the door. It was Detective Chief Inspector Stone.

He walked into the house without my asking. I didn't offer him a cup of tea.

'Why did you send me this note?'

He held it out to me, my own handwriting on the church notepaper.

I was taken aback by his accusatory tone. 'Because it happened. I thought it my duty to tell you.'

'We have made enquiries.' He walked around the room, looking at everything, staring into corners, in the way people do when they are buying your house. 'There is no one of this description employed as a gardener by the council. The gardeners, in any case, do not work on Saturdays. And the roses were pruned in February. No one had instructions to prune them this late in the season.'

I said, 'But the roses have been pruned. I looked at them myself. They were recently cut.'

'Why did you tell Mrs Marcus at the council offices that you had a pouch of his? Might I see this pouch?'

At this I blushed red. 'I'm sorry, there is no pouch. I'm afraid I made that up . . . a rather inept attempt to get some information, I'm afraid.'

He looked at me in that condescending way the police

have when they have you in the wrong and which I cannot stand. Vicars are not supposed to lie, not to anyone, not in any circumstances. I felt I had been caught with my pants down; even more because I stood here unshaven, in my dressing gown, my pyjama trousers sagging.

Stone walked across the room and looked out of the window.

'What is going on?' he asked me.

I said I didn't know what he meant.

'I am beginning to form the opinion that there is some strange conspiracy here to mislead and misinform the police,' he said. 'This is a very serious matter. A body is stolen from the mortuary and concealed. False reports are given to the police. Paintings are tampered with in order to give the appearance of the deceased.'

'Paintings tampered with?' I said, not understanding what he was talking about. 'This is extraordinary. Do you have any evidence? What can you mean by this?'

'If you wouldn't mind getting dressed and coming over to the church you will see.'

I went upstairs and dressed rapidly, pulling on my clothes with clumsy, unresponsive fingers. I went into the bathroom and quickly pulled a comb through my hair. It was receding in front and grey hairs were appearing at my temples. Until the age of forty I have to confess that I still felt as if I were twenty-five and that I was going to live for ever. The face staring back at me from the mirror gave the lie to that.

I went downstairs and accompanied the chief inspector across the road. The door of the church was open; who had opened it, I don't know. Inside, men were standing on a scaffold, tapping with tiny chisels and picking at the face of Christ on the painting of the baptism. I was beside myself. This was an outrage; surely this could not be done without permission?

'This is a house of God,' I said. 'This is an act of desecration. This is sacrilege!' Words could not express what I felt. To see these people scraping paint from the face of this beloved picture which I had faced every Sunday for the last five years, in front of which I had preached sermons and baptised children, filled me with rage. I was beside myself. 'How could you do this without permission?'

'But we have had permission.'

'From whom?'

'From the Archdeacon. We wrote to him, explaining that this was a criminal investigation, a murder. We needed to take samples of paint from the church, and of course permission was granted.'

'But why did you not inform me?' I could hear my voice rising to a childish squeak.

'A letter is in the post. It is regrettable that we had to start before it reached you.'

There was no disguising his contempt for me. I stood in the church, and tears came into my eyes. I was humiliated. I stood and watched the workers for a few moments. I would have asked them to stop but it was probably too late; the damage had been done. 'Please,' I said, 'be as careful as you can. This painting is a work of art.'

'We are taking every care,' said Stone. 'Now, if you have

a few moments, I would like a word with you in your office.'

We went through to my study. The blinds were drawn and it was cold and slightly damp. I sat on my chair. Stone sat opposite me.

'We are keeping an eye on everybody connected with this church,' he said. 'I don't know what motive you might have for such actions, but it's clear that anyone who could do these things must be deranged. Is there anyone in your congregation who might get involved in something like this? Some religious nutcase? Someone who might act out a dangerous fantasy, who might have ideas of grandeur, who might seek fame by proving the existence of miracles?'

His eyes bored into mine uncomfortably. I stared back into his. I am a good judge of souls, reflected in people's eyes; I am not sure that Stone had one. His eyes were all black, opaque, angry, hostile.

'I can see where your thoughts are leading,' I said, 'And I can see that it seems to offer a reasonable explanation. But there is no one in my church who would do such a thing.'

'We would like to interview all the members of your congregation.'

'I am sure you have the power to do so.'

'Will you co-operate?'

'As long as it is sensitively done.'

'I would like a list, then, of your regular attenders.'

His demands infuriated me. I strove to keep calm.

'Suppose the criminal were an irregular attender.'

'Then I would like a list of the names and addresses of everyone you know who has come to the church.'

'I could give you the circulation list for the parish magazine. It's about two hundred households.'

I reached into the file, took out the list, made a photocopy in the fax machine, and handed it to him. He eyed it suspiciously. 'This is everyone?'

'If I think of any others I can let you know.'

'You couldn't put a mark by the regular people?'

I went through the list and put a cross by some thirty or forty names.

Stone stood up. He looked at me with something pitifully approximating menace and said, 'As I said at the beginning, we'll get to the bottom of this, you can be sure of that.' I got the feeling that he already knew who his suspect was, that he wanted to let me know but didn't dare make any unsubstantiated accusations, and had to content himself with this rather feeble parting shot.

Well, it has got to him, too, I thought. Perhaps he is not a bad man. He wrote to me two days later saying that the samples of paint from the face of Christ showed that some of the paint was of a type different from the rest of the painting and had only recently been applied. I looked at that face every day and I did not believe that there was any change. I studied some old photographs and wrote to James Durfield; certainly he knew nothing about it. He told me he was very upset about the whole business, the police had come to visit him; his voice trembled on the phone.

Stone was accusing someone – possibly me – of fabricating evidence. Of course we know that the police have been accused of this themselves, especially locally, and particularly in relation to the planting of drugs on innocent people. Personally I would prefer to think that a policeman might fabricate evidence to provide a rational explanation for an event which otherwise might lead his superiors to think he had gone off his head, than that a churchgoer might feel the need to fabricate the passion and resurrection of Christ to restore his battered faith.

The Man in the Street

I was walking down Lavender Grove towards the vicarage when I suddenly had the strangest sensation that I was not alone, and that somebody was following me. Was it a shadow that I caught out of the corner of my eye, or the wind in a tree, or some slight sound that my ears had misinterpreted? I turned suddenly, as if I were playing a game of grandmother's footsteps, casting my eyes right down the street. There was no one there. The sun was shining brightly, and it was about midday, so there were no long shadows. The street was completely deserted; not a car, not a person. In fact, for an instant I felt as if time must have stood still, so powerful was this image of the empty street.

A cat emerged from one of the gardens up the road and walked slowly across the street, its tail pointing straight up in the air. A car ran across Malvern Road, heading south, and somebody came into view at the corner of the street, to pop a letter into the post-box.

I went on walking down the road, and, once more, I had the unmistakable feeling that there was someone walking behind me. Again, I looked round, and again, there was nobody there.

I came to the gate of the vicarage. My hand was shaking slightly as I pulled out my key and inserted it in the lock. I went inside, and shut the door firmly behind me. It was very quiet in the house; the children were at school and Harriet was teaching. I walked through into the kitchen and looked hopefully in the fridge.

There was nothing much there. I decided to make myself a sandwich and opened a bottle of beer. I took this through into my study and put the plate and the glass down on my desk.

I was facing the bookshelf, looking for an old copy of the Book of Common Prayer. I felt a shadow cross the room and, as I turned my head, I was sure I caught a glimpse of someone disappearing from the window.

I turned and darted through the hall, flinging open the front door. I glanced all around, but there was no one there. Was I going off my head? I looked down at the flower bed under the window, where the first green shoots of the peonies were emerging like little fingers from the earth. No, I was not imagining it. There were fresh footprints in the dark soil, not the children's but large footprints, from a man's heavy shoes.

I went back inside and returned to my desk. This time, I turned the chair round to face the window.

There was really no need for me to be so alarmed. Burglary rates in our area are very high. Most of the break-ins occur by day, when people are out working, and are entirely opportunistic. They come up to the house and peer in through the windows, and if there's no sign of anyone, they break a pane and are in and out in a minute. Of course, it is usual for them to ring the doorbell first. If someone answers, they make some lame excuse. If no one does, they know they are free to break in.

As I sat at my desk, the phone rang. It startled me so much that I jumped and my hand shot out and knocked the glass of beer on to the floor. I floundered, trying to retrieve it, while at the same time picking up the receiver.

'Hello? Hello?'

It was Kevin Brown, the journalist from the Hackney Gazette. He said that he had read my article in the parish magazine. Was this a true reflection of my views?

I said of course, I had written it, after all.

'So you think the resurrection is just a myth.'

'I said what I said in my article,' I replied, annoyed, dabbing the beer off the carpet with the corner of the table-cloth. 'Please don't try to misquote me. I said quite clearly at the end of the letter that I was carrying on in faith.'

'Faith in what?'

Some of the red dye had come off the tablecloth on to

the carpet. I had made things much worse than if I had left the beer to sink in, and I couldn't help thinking of what Harriet would say to me that evening. The journalist sharply repeated his question; and to my dismay I found myself quite unable to answer him.

The Fish Restaurant

As I was reading the local paper on Thursday to see if the journalist had written anything uncomplimentary about me, I saw that there had been another stabbing, on Kingsland Road, the victim a Kurd who had just left the Kurdish Men's Club. There is a Turkish football club not far away, and from time to time, as the police are only too aware, violence breaks out between the two groups. We are not very far from Kingsland Road; surely it was not impossible that the murders were connected as Kevin Brown had suggested to me.

Detective Chief Inspector Stone had obviously dismissed this possibility. Perhaps he had drawn a blank. Perhaps no one in that community would tell the police anything. Might I succeed in finding something out when they had failed?

I left my office early, leaving the answerphone on, and walked down to Kingsland Road. It was getting dark, and the sky was heavy and grey, looking like rain. The Kurdish Men's Club was near the traffic lights. Strong metal grilles had been secured over the windows and the door too was reinforced. A sign on the door said 'Members Only'.

I peered through a window and saw, through the metal grating, two tables covered in green cloth and a snooker table. Men sat at the tables reading newspapers and smoking, and another stood and played at a games machine.

The atmosphere was so strange and so foreign that I realised at once the futility of hoping that anyone would talk to me. This was so clear that I couldn't bring myself to enter.

'Looking for something, love?'

I turned round. Two girls were standing behind me, wearing short skirts, tight boots and layers of thick make-up. When one of the tarts saw my dog collar she nudged the other and burst out laughing.

I walked hurriedly down the street, wondering what to do. This thing was eating away at me; I must try to forget it. I should leave the investigation to the police, and try to put my own feelings to one side.

A little further down the road there is a well-known fish restaurant. It was now dark and cold outside, and had begun to rain, slow, feeble drops, as if even the weather were indecisive. My eye was drawn to the bright window, slightly fugged with steam. I felt hungry, and was wondering whether to get some fish and chips for supper, to save Harriet cooking. The rain suddenly started to fall in earnest, so without hesitating any longer I pushed the door open and walked into the shop.

The powerful smell of oil and chips assaulted me. I stood in the queue and looked around. And then I saw the man sitting at the table. His face was thin and sallow and there were dark hollows under his eyes. His skin seemed quite pale under the bright fluorescent lights, and I wondered why I had remembered it much darker and thought that he might be from the Middle East. I saw him sitting facing me, his mouth half open, and the forkful of white fish raised halfway to his lips.

His eyes fell upon me, and I am sure that he recognised me when our eyes met, otherwise, wouldn't he have looked away? He didn't smile, or blink, or nod, or acknowledge me in any way, but simply regarded me with his even, detached gaze. Then, almost as if he were mocking me, he popped the white morsel of fish into his mouth.

I saw him chew and then swallow. I turned in confusion and rushed out of the shop. I found myself walking down the road, almost stumbling in confusion. My limbs felt heavy and my head felt light. I wondered what on earth was happening to me.

What was the reason for this fear? I was sure this was not a hallucination. There was undoubtedly another man, who looked like the man who had died. There must be some connection between them. Perhaps that was why he was hanging around here, wanting to avenge his death.

There was no doubt that there could be danger; real, physical danger, not something imagined, and this could be responsible for the overpowering terror that I felt. If the man recognised me, and knew that I was watching him, then might I not be actually at risk?

As I walked, pulling my jacket collar up to protect me from the driving rain, I saw two policemen walking down the road. I pulled out of my pocket the newspaper photograph of the man, the one I had intended to show to the men in the Kurdish Men's Club. I went up to them and told them I had just seen someone sitting in the fish restaurant who looked exactly like this man. Perhaps it was a coincidence, but couldn't it be that he was a relative?

The police officers obviously knew about the murder, and I suppose they also knew that Stone was desperate for leads. I realised that my jacket collar was pulled up around my neck, and that they didn't know who I was, and that perhaps that was a relief. They thanked me and walked off, and I saw them step into the restaurant. I followed them back, and stood outside, looking in through the window. I saw the policemen go up to the man, and I saw his eyes turn to look out of the window, and stare in my direction.

The Evening in the Vicarage

Could he see me in the darkness? I couldn't tell. I turned and walked away at once. Remorse suddenly swept over me, as if I had betrayed him. But this was nonsense. Of course, the police couldn't harm him. What could they do? They couldn't arrest him for sitting in a restaurant and looking like someone who had been killed.

When I got home, wet and bedraggled, Harriet was waiting for me. She was angry that I hadn't told her where I was, and reminded me that it was several nights since I'd been there to eat with them and help her get the children ready for bed.

She put the supper on the table in front of me and turned to face me. We looked at one another for a moment. From upstairs came the sound of one of the children wailing. She gave an impatient gesture and was about to go when I said, 'I'll go up.'

'They've been rowing all afternoon. It's mostly Tom's fault.'

I ran upstairs and found Joshua howling at the top of the stairs. He said, between sobs, that Tom had hidden his monkey and wouldn't tell him where it was. Joshua is unable to go to sleep without his monkey. I went into the room and found Tom sitting on the top bunk, grinning all over his face.

'I hid it this morning but I've forgotten where. I just can't remember.'

I was tired and ill at ease and I have to confess I felt like hitting him. It's a sad truth, but Thomas has tormented Joshua mercilessly from the moment he was born. I see other families who deny that they have any problem with sibling rivalry and I simply can't believe it. Nothing is more irritating than listening to mothers saying, 'Oh, she's not jealous,' while on the other side of the sofa their toddler is hugging the baby with such ferocity that it has to be rescued.

'Well, you'd better remember quickly,' I said, looking around the room, in the drawers and cupboards, under the bed.

'But I've been trying to remember,' said Tom, still with that infuriating smile on his face. Joshua, standing in the doorway, began to wail with renewed vigour. Copious hot tears trickled down his face.

Suddenly I couldn't be bothered with the whole charade; I didn't want to waste hours of my time looking for the monkey, I wanted to be downstairs with Harriet, whom I had hardly seen for a week. I walked across to the bed, and my expression must have been so alarming that Thomas gave a shriek and threw himself under the bedclothes. I grabbed him and pulled him out, squealing from the pain of my hand biting into his upper arm. 'Tell me where you put that monkey,' I said, still struggling to be calm, 'or there'll be no television for a week.'

'I don't want to watch television.'

Something in me snapped. It was his insolent, irritating expression that did it. 'Tell me where you hid the monkey!' I took hold of his hair, and pulled and twisted it. 'Tell me at once!'

Thomas started to wail now, but refused to say anything. I pulled his hair harder and then he suddenly said, 'In the airing cupboard!' I abruptly let go and went into the airing cupboard, and pulled out the monkey from behind the tank. Joshie grabbed it and immediately stopped crying, but now Thomas was wailing from the room. 'It's not fair! Why don't you hit him! You never hit him!'

I went back into the bedroom, my rage suddenly replaced by an overwhelming feeling of shame. Why did we wonder that people tortured or did violence to one another? If I could hurt my children, whom I loved more than myself, what couldn't I do to a stranger?

I calmed the children down and said a prayer quickly

with them. Tom had stopped crying and I kissed them both tenderly. I went downstairs, sat back at the table, and put my head in my hands.

Harriet stood and looked at me. She said, 'Richard, you're not usually like this. There's something wrong. Can't you tell me what's the matter with you?'

I stared at her, numbly. What could I say? I took a deep breath.

'Harriet, I saw this man again, the one we saw in Clissold Park, in the fish restaurant in Kingsland Road.'

She looked at me, puzzled. 'So?' She sat down opposite me, and put her hand on my arm. 'Richard, I was thinking about the stolen body,' she said. 'Couldn't it be drugs? Perhaps he was carrying drugs, had swallowed them in plastic bags, or something like that.'

I said, 'I'm sure the police would have thought of that. But if there had been drugs on the body, they would have been found at the post mortem. Surely the police would have said something about it by now?'

'Would they?'

I stared at Harriet. She had a point. I supposed that the police would only release the information if it suited them. I am not very well versed in the working of the police, what they choose to release, and who controls this. Suddenly I felt I had to know what had happened to the man in the restaurant; I picked up the phone and rang Detective Chief Inspector Stone.

By a stroke of luck he was still there. He listened to me impatiently.

'Yes, the officers did tell me about the incident. I should have guessed that it was you behind it.'

'Did they find out who the man was?'

He sighed. 'Listen. You don't seem to realise what little power we have. We can ask the man for his identity, but he doesn't have to tell us, and, for your information, this guy didn't. We can't force him to say anything, and we can't arrest him on suspicion of looking a little bit like someone else, now, can we?' He paused and exhaled deeply, as if he were smoking a cigarette. 'Of course, if we had identity cards, it would be different.'

'So you don't intend to find out who he is?'

'No. To be frank with you, I think it would be a complete waste of our time.'

I could sense that he was trying very hard to be polite, so I thanked him, and hung up. I thought again of the man in the fish restaurant, and the expression on his face. Harriet was hovering behind me. 'Richard, you're shaking. What is it?' she asked.

But I simply couldn't explain to her what was bothering me most; what the man had been eating. For in Luke when the resurrected Christ appears to the disciples, in order to prove he is not a ghost, he sits down with them, and before their eyes consumes a piece of broiled fish.

The Discovery in the Vestry

Every year, usually in April or May, the Archdeacon comes to visit the churchwardens and make sure everything is ship-shape. His visitation is normally concerned with such mundane matters as money management, dealing with the weekly offertory and church insurance, ensuring that the gutters aren't leaking and so on. Normally the churchwardens rush around beforehand making sure the silver is polished, the vestry neat and tidy, that the grass in the garden has been mown and the weeds pulled out of the paving in front of the porch.

At the bottom of the form to be completed by the churchwardens is a space in which they can, in confidence, state any problems that they feel they have with the church, its congregation or its present incumbent. Despite my mood of depression at the time, I had no reason to think that there would be any problem.

Before the visitation we decided to do some spring cleaning, and, in particular, to clean out the cupboards in the vestry. The two churchwardens, Chris Shaw and Mercy, were in charge, and Sidney had also agreed to help us.

We were emptying out the back of the old wardrobe. There we found a pile of ancient prayerbooks, some old costumes for a nativity play, and a box of long-forgotten hymnsheets. At the back we found a box of acrylic artist's paints.

'What were these used for?' I asked, picking through them. They were large, expensive tubes, mostly unused, and I was surprised that someone would have forgotten them.

'Oh, I remember,' said Sidney. 'It was before your time, Richard. The ceiling leaked in that storm and a bit of the painting got damaged. A local artist came and touched it up.'

'Which painting? Not the baptism?'

Sidney nodded.

'Do you know who the artist was?'

'No, I can't rightly remember.'

I felt at once a sense of great relief and excitement; this at least explained the findings of Detective Chief Inspector Stone. It was partly my fault that I hadn't found out about this, as, in my shame, I hadn't told anyone about the accusations of the police. I said that I would take them to my office and try to find out who they belonged to. I could ring my predecessor; almost certainly he would know who the artist was.

Mercy grabbed hold of me as I turned to go. 'Richard, I've been meaning to ask you; did you go to Clissold Park, like you said you would? Did you see this man?' When I didn't answer, she went on, 'What do you think Mary saw, Richard? Do you think it was a vision?'

Chris said, 'I think this kind of talk is dangerous. It's getting out of hand . . . you two are not the only people who claim to have seen him.'

'Who else are you talking about?' I asked, astonished, pausing in the doorway with the box of paints.

Mercy carried on calmly emptying the cupboard. 'Gordon says he saw the man walking in London Fields. And that family who were staying here, they saw him too, they say.'

Chris put a box down on the floor. 'I think you should say something, Richard,' he said, 'to put a stop to this. It could be very bad for the church if the press get hold of it.'

'Why?' I asked.

'Well, Mary is already saying that it means there's some special significance in this church, that we've been singled out for some kind of miracle . . . quite frankly it isn't healthy.'

'She hasn't said anything more to me about it.'

'That's because she said you don't believe her,' said Mercy, putting down the dustpan and brush.

'That's not true. I do believe her.'

'What?' Chris straightened up from the cupboard and looked me straight in the eye. 'Believe what, exactly?'

I felt that to stand here and listen to this conversation, to take part in it, and not admit anything, would be dishonest. 'Because I went up to Clissold Park and saw the same thing as she did.'

'So you have seen Him?' exclaimed Mercy, throwing up her hands in delight. 'Praise the Lord!'

Chris stood and stared at me, his eyes wide with what looked like horror. Suddenly I realised that I had made a great error. I excused myself, and said that I had some urgent phone calls to make, and that they could find me in my office if they needed me.

I shut the door firmly behind me, sat at my desk and tried to think clearly. I, too, felt that this whole thing could have a serious effect in dividing the congregation. But what could I say? I was more in doubt about what was going on than anyone.

I looked down at the box of paints. I felt it was my clear duty to inform the police about this discovery, and to try to trace the local artist. I went through the church files, finally finding an insurance claim concerning the leak of water through the roof which occurred in the hurricane of October 1987, just before I came to St Michael's. I photocopied this and attached it to a letter saying I was trying to trace the artist, which I promptly dispatched to Detective Chief Inspector Stone.

✝essa

Tessa has been the deaconess at our church for the past three years. She is a passionate believer in women's ordination. Now that the first women have become priests, it is her firm intention to follow in their footsteps. This will inevitably mean leaving us, an event which I must confess I do not look forward to. In the meantime she continues to be a great support to me and everybody in the church.

On Saturday morning she came to see me in my study in great distress and told me she had been visited by the police. She told me that she had been intimidated by their questioning and that they had asked her many searching questions about me. It seemed they had found out that I had visited a psychotherapist while at university, and that my mother had killed herself when in a deep depression following the birth of her second child, my brother Philip. To cut it short, she said, they wanted to know if I was also going off my head.

I must confess that when she said this I was afraid. The police might be asking such questions of the Archdeacon, even the Bishop. They might be talking to other priests, to people in the community, raising doubts about me, blackening my name. I was in real fear that this might get out of hand, that Stone was pursuing a personal vendetta against me.

Yet surely I could defend myself? I believed myself to be popular in the parish. And yet, thinking about it, I was no longer sure. I was certainly too wishy-washy for those in the congregation who liked to take the Bible more literally than I did. Perhaps my approach was not sound enough for the intellectuals. It was quite possible that in trying to satisfy the needs and viewpoints of all the vastly different people in my congregation I was pleasing no one. Chris's reaction to my admission that I too had seen the man in Clissold Park was also worrying. In short, my position might not be as secure as I had thought.

'Tell me truthfully, Tessa,' I said, reaching over and taking her hand, 'How do the congregation feel about me? Do they think that I'm doing a good job? Do they have faith in me?'

'Oh, absolutely. I am sure of it. How can you doubt yourself? You are a wonderful priest.'

'Tessa, are you sure of this?'

'Of course.'

'And if you heard anything to the contrary, would you tell me? Any rumour, any small thing I've done to offend, however trivial?'

'I promise.' She was staring into my face, her cheeks pale, her eyes searching mine. Tessa was not a beautiful woman. Her face was rather thin, austere, with heavy eyes. She gave me a look of such intimacy that I forgot for an instant who I was with, and somehow, in my mind, I felt I was with Harriet, who was the only other woman who had ever been so close and looked at me like that. Instinctively I took her face in my hands and kissed her. It was not exactly a sexual kiss, but it was not exactly a chaste one either.

Tessa looked at me with amazement and for an instant something like a smile played on her lips. Realizing what I had done, I instantly released her, dropping my hands from her face like two heavy stones. She jumped back from me at once. Her cheeks flamed red; she murmured in confusion and then she fled from the room, leaving me alarmed and alone.

To Abney Park Cemetery

I sat and stared at the floor. Something truly terrible was happening to me. I felt for a moment that I was losing my sanity, that I was sliding into a dark pit. The cross stood on the window-ledge, mocking me. Unable to sit there, I stood up and walked out into the street. Although the sun was shining I felt as if a cloud had passed across its face and left everything dark and cold. I got into the car and began to drive, I don't know where. I made a desperate attempt to pray, what I called 'arrow prayers', little darts of prayer fired at heaven, but I couldn't.

I drove west, turned the car at Essex Road and drove north towards Stoke Newington. Then I turned east and drove to Kingsland Road. I thought I might go for a walk in Abney Park cemetery. I turned north again and drove into Church Street, parked the car in a side road and walked through the wrought iron gates into the cemetery. Although it was early May it was quite cold again, though the blossom was out and the leaves starting to show on the trees.

I walked down the great avenue of trees with the new buds opening and pale green light shining down through them. On the ground, ivy and brambles grew everywhere, smothering the tombstones, many of which were broken and tilted to one side as if the dead were pushing up from underneath. I wandered among the big Victorian monuments, topped with angels and engraved with tragic verse. A battered angel looked down on me, its face smeared with graffiti. Ivy sprawled over the stone and, next to it, a statue bowed its head under a generous sprinkling of bird droppings.

In one grave lay buried a young mother and her child. Another read 'Our first dear baby, Cyril, aged two and a half years: Thine angel has sung thee to sleep.' I remembered our first dead daughter and Harriet's grief at her loss and suddenly sat down there, weeping.

The man walked past me down the path. I saw at once that it was him. I stood up, without an instant's hesitation, and began to follow him. He was dressed in jeans and a shabby jacket, was carrying a newspaper, and wore a pair of threadbare gloves on his hands. He wore old trainers, which made no sound, and his movements were easy and fluid like an athlete's.

I followed him along the narrow, overgrown paths, between the gravestones. In the spring sunlight I saw that he cast a shadow. He turned left, where the ruined chapel stood with its crenellated tower, and walked under the big iron gate. I followed, nervously, anxious not to lose him, but not wanting to come too close.

Corrugated iron covered the empty windows and inside it was very dark. Feathers and bird droppings coated the floor and two pigeons flapped noisily under the roof. The place was ominous and smelt of the stale urine of tramps who had sheltered there. There was no sign at all of the man.

I walked gratefully out into the daylight. Then I saw him again, standing in the sunshine not far away, pausing to read the messages on the wreaths on a newly dug grave. Then he turned and began to walk away again, at the same easy, relaxed pace. The words in Luke came suddenly into my mind; 'Why search among the dead for one who is living?'

He walked steadily towards the exit on Church Street, showing no signs of noticing me. I followed him to the bus-stop, keeping my distance, and glancing about as I went in an effort to seem casual. Near the bus-stop was a newsagent. I looked up the road to check that no bus was in sight, popped in, and bought an Evening Standard. I went back to the bus-stop, leaning against the wall, burying my face in the paper.

After five or six minutes the bus came, screeching to a halt; I felt the hot breath from the engine. The man walked to the front of the bus and sat down. I sat behind him. I was so close that I could reach out and touch his shoulder. Part of me wanted to do so, just to check that he was real, that my hand wouldn't simply pass through the fabric of his body like an image on a screen. His hair was thick and unkempt, slightly longer than it had been on the day he staggered to the church. When he turned his head slightly to look out of the window I caught a glimpse of his profile and the thin, almost arrogant nose.

The bus headed south towards Dalston. At Shacklewell Lane he got off and I followed him. He walked down the road towards St Mark's Rise, and into a big, four-storey Victorian house on the left-hand side going down the hill. The big black-painted door slammed shut behind him.

I stood out on the street. The nearby church clock struck twelve. I walked up the steps and peered at the doorbells. It was divided into multiple flats and there were seven bells in all. There were three names, Finnigan, Jones and Zadrack. The other bells had labels which were faded, torn or missing altogether.

I went down the steps and looked back at the house. The window sills were chipped and cracked and there were dingy curtains at the windows. One room I could see was a kitchen, and bottles of washing-up liquid and cleaning fluid were lined along the window frame with a couple of faded-looking plants. On the top floor I saw somebody drawing back a curtain.

The door opened suddenly and a girl stepped out. She had long black hair, was wearing a short leather skirt, short jacket and a bright red scarf wrapped round her neck. She had high boots with complicated fastenings and a lot of make-up on her face. She came down the steps, walking with exaggerated care along the pavement, then she stopped and lit a cigarette. She stood by the wall and put out a hand to steady herself, and as she did so she dropped the cigarette packet. She leaned over and her bag swung forward and hit her leg, causing her to sway on the high heels. I stepped towards her and picked up the cigarettes, handing them to her.

Her arms were long and thin and scarred at the wrists when she put out her hand to me. Her face could have been pretty but the skin was bad, coarse and pock-marked under her make-up. She looked at me oddly. She asked, 'Are you from the church?'

'Not this church.' I took a step back from her. 'Um . . . I was wondering if you could help me . . . somebody said they were in a spot of trouble and asked me to go and see them. This was the address but there's no name on the bell . . . a Mr Spencer.'

'Spencer? No, I don't know. There's me, there's Sarah and Angie, there's the Polish guy with the wife and baby, Mr Finnigan, he's not here, he's in hospital again, and then there's Mr and Mrs Rose . . . and then there's the guy on the top floor.'

'Could he be Mr Spencer?'

She looked at me and laughed. 'No, I don't think he could be Mr Spencer.'

'Is he about thirty, with dark hair, a bit long, a nose like this . . .?'

'You know him?' She was startled.

'I just saw him going in the house.'

'You're a bit nosy, aren't you?' She turned away suddenly and began walking down the street. I watched her go. I looked at the clock; I would be late for lunch, and although I was only a ten or fifteen minute walk from home, I had to go and collect the car first.

I rang Harriet from a payphone to say I would be a bit late. Her voice sounded distant and odd.

'You'd better come home at once,' she said. 'Tessa's been here.'

The Trouble with Harriet

When I got home Harriet had not made lunch and the boys had gone to play with a neighbour. Harriet was sitting in the garden smoking. Her hand was shaking, not quite steady, and her face looked white and hard.

'Harriet,' I began, knowing what was coming, 'It's all a misunderstanding.'

'I don't see how it could be.'

'I did kiss her,' I said, 'I can't explain why, I forgot myself. We were talking very honestly together and . . . somehow I got mixed up in my mind and thought it was you.'

How could anyone have said anything more pathetic and incomprehensible? I could hear as I said the words how absurd they sounded. 'Me?' she echoed back at me. She stared at me, as if I were crazy. 'How could you possibly think that Tessa was me?'

'I can't explain. I was distracted. She was sitting there, in front of me . . .'

She interrupted me. 'Tessa has told me everything.'

'Everything?'

'Yes, everything. How she has been in love with you for two years. How she's tried to conceal it, to keep her position in the parish. How she realised, finally, that you felt the same way about her. That she didn't want to hurt me, that she couldn't let us face the scandal, and how she is resigning from the parish at once.'

I sat down on the chair next to her. This was a disaster. How could I have seen it coming? It had never occurred to me that the warmth Tessa had always shown towards me was anything other than an expression of her loving and generous nature. In the church it was normal to be physically demonstrative, to hug and kiss one another. How could I explain myself to Harriet? Surely she would listen when I tried to explain?

'I knew,' said Harriet, 'that there was something the matter with you. All this time you've been so secretive, not telling me where you were going, what you were doing, going around in a daze, being impatient with the children. I knew that there was something the matter, but I thought it might have been to do with the murder. I know that upset you terribly, that you might have been having doubts, lost your faith, that kind of thing. I didn't want to trouble you, I've always trusted you, I knew that if I gave you enough time you would come to me and tell me what was the matter. But I never imagined that it could be anything like this.'

Her voice, which she had kept under control, now broke and tears flooded her eyes. She put her hand in front of her face, her lips trembled, and she buried her face in her hands, leaning forward over the table. The teacup was knocked from its saucer and fell on to the stone terrace where it smashed into tiny fragments. It was her own special cup, that had come from her grandmother, the very last of the set, but she seemed not even to have noticed.

'Harriet,' I said, 'Harriet.' I put my hand on her shoulder. 'Harriet, it's not true that I love Tessa. I think it's true that she's got a thing about me, I realise that now, I should have seen it before, but I don't think I've ever done or said anything that would give her the impression that I returned her feelings. And I don't return them. Harriet, this is terrible. The last thing I could ever want is to hurt you.'

'Go away. Don't touch me! You are odious.'

'Harriet!'

She leapt to her feet. She was wearing a close-fitting dress and a string of beads and I noticed the sun brought out red highlights in her hair. She must have had it hennaed the other day when she went to the hairdresser's and I hadn't even noticed. She turned and ran back into the house. I followed her in terror. 'Harriet!' I yelled. 'Harriet!'

She ran upstairs and locked the door to our bedroom. I bolted up the stairs behind her and pounded on the door. I have always had a terror of locked doors. My mother had locked the door when she killed herself and I had been unable to get into the room. She did it because of my father's infidelity; I had understood nothing of it at the time, and my father afterwards held that she had only done it so as to render the rest of his life intolerable. I can remember standing there, banging and banging and my mother not answering, and finally lying down to cry on the landing till my father came home.

'Harriet,' I said, in desperation, 'You can't do this. Open the door or I'll break it down!'

She opened the door and looked at me. We were both crying. She suddenly took hold of me and we clung to one another, sank down on the bed, and sobbed in one another's arms. I stroked her hair and soothed her like a child and said all kinds of things, I can't remember, that I would never leave her, that I would never be unfaithful, that I would never love anybody else. I think that she believed me.

In the silence that followed this storm of emotion, I also told her that I had seen the man again and followed him to his house.

The House in St Mark's Rise

Harriet had told me that what I was doing was dangerous, that I must not become obsessed. She was afraid that I would stumble into something evil. Harriet does not believe in evil. She always says that human beings are capable of anything and the extraordinary thing is not that so many awful things happen in the world but that these things tend to happen rather less often than one might expect. So for her to use this word meant that she was very frightened indeed.

On Sunday Tessa was at the church well before the service. I asked her to come into my office. I said that I had kissed her because I was so very fond of her and that her support had meant so much to me over the years we had worked together. I said that I didn't love her in the way that she hoped and that I loved only Harriet, that I understood why she had said what she had to Harriet and that I had perhaps not behaved quite properly towards her in the past, that Harriet and I had talked it all over and that everything was all right between us, and that I hoped she would not resign, at least not immediately.

I think that I handled it rather well.

In the afternoon, after lunch, Harriet took the children off to visit some friends. I said I was feeling stressed, there was a lot of paperwork that I had left unattended for too long, and I would rather stay behind to catch up with things. Harriet tried to persuade me to go with her, and I asked her if it was because she didn't trust me. I gave her my word that I was not staying behind to see Tessa. When they had gone I sat in my office and waded through bills and letters but the time dragged terribly. I felt hot and restless, almost ill. I decided to take a walk in the fresh air and perhaps drop in on somebody.

It was a warm afternoon. I took off my jacket as I walked, and swung along at a brisk pace and soon, almost before I realised it, I was in St Mark's Rise.

I looked at the house. I went up to the door and rang a bell, one of the unlabelled ones. At once my heart started pounding. There was another bell and I rang that. A woman in her sixties came to the door.

'I've come to see the young man upstairs.'

'Oh, yes, of course,' she said, looking at me with the

respect I often encountered from people of that age. 'That's all right, vicar. Come in.'

She went back into her own flat and I went up the stairs. The carpet was old and frayed and the wallpaper was dirty and scratched and slightly mouldy. Someone was playing music loudly on the second floor and there was a stale smell of fried food on the staircase.

The door to the top flat was ajar. I knocked on it.

Nobody came. I knocked again, louder. Then I pushed the door open and walked into the flat.

Afternoon sunlight was coming into the room through the grimy windows and it dappled the walls. They had been painted white, quite recently. The floorboards were bare, dark, old wood, unvarnished, and there was a small worn rug on the floor. The room contained some cushions and a futon-style mattress on the floor, an old table and chairs of the sort you might get out of a skip, roughly mended, and a bookcase crammed with books. I went over and looked at them. There were books on Buddhism, Judaism and Christian philosophy, works by St John of the Cross and Julian of Norwich, a Bible, the Penguin Quran, a book on Sufism and Eastern mysticism, Evelyn Underhill's *Mysticism*, *The Cloud of Unknowing*, *The Dead Sea Scrolls*, the sermons of Meister Eckhart and *The Myth of God Incarnate*. On the shelf stood a little crucifix, a candle, and a small statue of the Buddha. A joss stick had been burned and there was still a faint scent of it on the air. The room had that atmosphere that you could sense, that someone prayed here. It was very strong.

The room was divided from a tiny kitchen by a curtain. In the kitchen were some shelves, an old cooker, and a white enamel sink. Above the sink was a cracked mirror and a shelf, and that was all.

I went to the table and opened its one drawer. There was nowhere else to put papers or any personal effects. The drawer contained some blank pieces of paper and some banknotes but nothing more. I slid it shut silently. I walked around the room but there were no papers there at all, no bills, none of the usual letters or documents. There was nothing in the room to identify him at all.

I was about to go out when I heard footsteps on the stairs. My heart thumped; I couldn't stay, but then I couldn't go either. Perhaps the people were going into another flat. I hid behind the curtain and waited. There were voices, talking quietly, and the footsteps came on steadily until finally they came into the room.

I shrank back against the wall, but found that I could see quite clearly through a small tear in the curtain. It was the man, dressed in a black shirt and trousers, and with him was the girl. She was wearing a man's old dressing gown in a dull kind of brown. It was too big for her and suited her much better than the leather outfit she had worn the other day. Her hair was loose and she looked prettier than before, especially in the soft sunlight coming through the window. They stood in the centre of the room and looked at one another.

He gestured to her and she slipped off the dressing gown. She was wearing nothing underneath. She was a big-boned girl but too thin, and her skin was very pale; her arms were knotted with needle marks and there was a scar on her lower belly, probably from a Caesarean. Naked and with no make-up she looked vulnerable and almost shy. Opposite her, the man took off his shirt. Then he slipped off his trousers. He took her by her shoulders, then he turned her round, so that her back was towards me, and he was standing there, against the light, so that I couldn't see his features clearly.

He bent and kissed her. Then he stepped forward and sat down on the corner of the futon. Now the light was shining on his torso and I could see two scars, one of them running from the breastbone round under his arm, and a second starting at the throat and running down to the navel. The scars were red and puckered and together made the form of a cross. As he put his arms around her back, I could see that the hands were marked with red, puckered lines, like a spider.

I knew that what I was seeing was impossible and yet there I was, seeing it. This man was the same man, he had been dead, and now was living. Not only was he alive and able to walk in the fresh air, to talk and breathe, he was so quick that he was capable of sex. I could see his erect penis, standing out from his body, and the vigour that ran through him. He sat on the bed with his knees apart, and invited her to come and sit astride him.

I knew that I should not have looked at this. After a few moments I lowered my eyes. I felt dizzy, and there was a buzzing in my ears. I was so afraid that I thought I would faint and be discovered. I wanted to run past them, but I was afraid to. I thought that if she saw me the woman might go to the police. Stone would love it. I could see the headlines: PEEPING TOM VICAR IN TART'S FLAT. Yet how could I avoid discovery? I pulled back deeper behind the curtain. I thought of Polonius's death, and wondered if the same dramatic and justified end would come to me. The woman was moaning, the man cried out, and I heard their heavy breathing. I put my hands over my ears, but I couldn't blot it out, standing there overwhelmed by a terrible mixture of desire and shame.

After a while the sounds came to an end. There was a long period of peacefulness, and then I heard someone moving barefoot around the room. I heard a match strike, and then, after a pause, a whiff of incense. I heard a soft male voice ask, 'Would you like some tea?'

She murmured something. He came into the kitchen. It was getting dark now and the room was in deep shadow. I was afraid that he would switch on the light, and that then I would have no hope of concealing myself. But he lit the gas under a saucepan of water and went back into the room. I heard her say, 'Have you got anything to eat?'

'No, there's nothing.'

'I'll go down and get something. Do you want to come and help me carry it up?'

I heard the rustle of clothes being pulled on, footsteps on the floor, and then on the stairs. There was silence. I had to hope that both of them had gone, that he was not sitting there, silent, in the gathering darkness. I peeped out from behind the curtain. The room was empty. I tip-toed to the top of the stairs, but there was no one there. I walked cautiously down, past a half-open door on the landing from which light spilled, and down into the dark gloom of the entrance hall. I fumbled with the door catch, let myself out and closed the door quietly behind me.

I was soaked with sweat, and the cool evening breeze made me shiver. I walked down the street, half stumbling in the dark. One or two people looked at me oddly as I went past them. I was mad with fear and shame and couldn't understand what was going to happen to me. I tried to pray, but couldn't, because I had no image in my mind of anyone to pray to. Was I to pray to this young man in the house? Who, or what, was God or Christ? I was filled with emptiness.

I tried to think clearly. I should resign from my position, that was plain. God was not real for me, I couldn't pray to him for help or understanding, he had become for me a mere cipher, something meaningless, terrifying, hostile even. I thought that I should go and see a doctor, and that Harriet and I should go away at once, perhaps to her parents, for a week or two, until I felt better.

She was waiting for me in the hallway. I could have sworn that when I entered she was wringing her hands. She said, 'Oh God, where have you been? I nearly called the police.'

I was horrified at the implications of this. I said, 'You must never, never, call the police.'

'Why?'

'Because they are not to be trusted.'

'Richard, you are ill.'

'Yes, yes, I think I am ill, Harriet. I feel terrible. I think I am getting the flu.'

She came up and put her hand on my forehead. Then she said, quickly, 'Go up to bed. Do you want to eat anything? I can get you some soup.'

I took her hand in mine and pressed it against my cheek. I said, 'Bless you, Harriet, you are my salvation.' I went upstairs and started to run a bath. At the side of the bath were the children's toys, a plastic duck, a boat, a bobbing apple, a frog. They were all so familiar, so comforting. The door to the airing cupboard was hanging open and inside were the piles of towels, the children's clothes, the bedding, neatly folded. I leaned forward and put my head under the tap to feel the sensation of the water rushing over me.

Harriet came up with the soup and put me to bed. She tucked me in like a child and lay down beside me, and in a little while I was asleep.

The Archdeacon's Visit

In the morning when I woke I could hear the children downstairs. Harriet was rushing around, looking for shoes and library books, picking up the children's coats, getting ready to hurry them into the car. She paused in her frantic maternal round to come to me and kiss me on the cheek and ask me gently if I felt better. Before I could form an answer she was gone; the door banged behind her and there was silence. I went into the kitchen and poured some tea. I sat at the table staring out of the window, confused and alone, and decided I had some serious thinking to do.

The telephone rang. I hesitated to answer it, to face demands for support from other people when I was so desperately needing support myself. I let it ring six or seven times and then I picked it up.

It was the Archdeacon. He said he would be passing by my church later that morning and wondered if I would be free so that he could drop in and see me.

I consulted the diary. I had an appointment with an elderly parishioner which I could easily change. Of course, I could with all truth tell him I had a previous appointment and that I was very sorry, I wouldn't be there. But that was no good. The Archdeacon clearly wanted to see me quite urgently for a reason and it was much better to see him now rather than have it hanging over me.

I said that I would be in my office and that I would be delighted to see him.

I wondered what exactly had happened. Probably someone from the church had gone to see him. It could have been Tessa, perhaps out of wounded pride, though I could scarcely believe that of her; it could have been someone else, one of the wardens, perhaps Chris, who, following my remark in the vestry, seemed to think I had gone off my head. Or the congregation might have noticed my depression, my lack of fervour, my forgetfulness, even come to sense my lack of faith. Perhaps people had seen me wandering the streets, distracted, or they might have been influenced by Detective Chief Inspector Stone.

I took hold of myself and went to work in my study. There were a dozen messages on the answerphone and as many more unanswered from last week. I sorted out the urgent ones and began to make some calls. As I made the calls I began to feel better. Not doing this had been weigh-

ing heavily on my mind even though I hadn't been con-
sciously aware of it.

At twelve o'clock the Archdeacon came. He is a little
younger than me, a very tall, good-looking, energetic man,
and I have always got on with him perfectly well. We
chatted for a few moments, the usual polite enquiries into
family and church affairs, and then he settled himself
more comfortably in his chair.

He told me that after the visitation one of the churchwardens had said that they were not satisfied that I
believed enough in God or Christ to lead the congregation.
Members of the church had been upset by what they took
to be a lack of faith. One person in particular had said that
they came to me to ask for guidance after having a
religious experience and been more or less told that they
had imagined it.

I knew at once from this who it was and what had happened. I was filled with guilt that I had said nothing to
Mary about my own experiences, because, of course, I
doubted their reality. I thought that I was going mad, and
that, by implication, so was she.

It had never really occurred to me to think of this as a
collective hallucination. Had a similar event occurred
among Christ's disciples? I had been afraid even to discuss
this with anyone else, with Mary, with Tessa.

The Archdeacon cleared his throat.

'I understand, of course,' he said, 'that a very terrible
event occurred here in this church on Good Friday. I read
reports of it in the paper and I understand that the whole
affair is something of a mystery.'

I nodded.

'I understand that there hasn't been a great deal of publicity about the case, despite its obviously sensational aspects, and that the police haven't made a great deal of progress with their investigations. Recently I had a visit from Detective Chief Inspector Stone. He told me he had a theory that this whole thing had been organised deliberately to try and gain publicity for the church. He hinted that you might have been aware of this.'

'Has it occurred to you,' I said, trying to be reasonable and not angry, 'that the whole of the Christian story might have been based upon a similar hoax? After all, there is plenty of evidence to show that Jesus knew about, even provoked, his death on the cross. Plenty of people have speculated that the disciples themselves stole the body from the tomb.'

The Archdeacon looked at me, puzzled. It was clear he didn't understand why I was saying this.

'Is this what you believe?' I asked him.

'That the disciples stole the body? No, of course not.'

'You have no real evidence that this might not be true. Yet, on the basis of even less evidence, you might, for example, be prepared to think this of me.'

The Archdeacon brushed this aside. 'Oh come now, I think we know one another well enough. Nobody is making any accusations against you.'

'Aren't they?' I got up from my chair and sat down on the edge of my desk. I don't know why, but this made me feel more comfortable, perhaps because I was now looking down on the Archdeacon rather than him looking down on me. 'Isn't Chief Inspector Stone making exactly this kind of allegation?'

The Archdeacon was silent for a moment. 'I don't think so. I think he's just testing the waters. He asked me for a character reference, as it were, and I spoke of you very highly. But it does seem to me that this business has got you into a spot of trouble. I am talking of things spiritual, you understand.'

I didn't want to admit to him that what I felt was anything out of the ordinary. Why should I? Each of us is playing a role. 'But aren't we all in spiritual trouble? How many of us really know what we believe? We ask ourselves to accept miracles which took place two thousand years ago, when people did not understand medicine or science, when they believed that death simply meant the departure of the spirit from the body and that this spirit could, in exceptional circumstances, return. If we cannot believe in the miracles, as most of us can't, we look at their symbolic meaning and try to find a meaning in that. But what if the miracles are true? None of us has any faith. I tell you, if Jesus Christ himself came through that door right now, you would not believe it!'

He sat in silence, startled. I paused, pointing with emphasis at the door. Both of us turned and looked at it. It was a plain, modern door, painted blue, and there was nothing remarkable about it. But for a minute it seemed to me that the air moved behind it, the door swung inwards slightly, and that something hovered behind it in the corridor.

I got to my feet and looked outside. No one was there.

I closed the door behind me firmly and went back to sit on the edge of my desk.

The Archdeacon cleared his throat. 'Well, what I have been trying to say is that perhaps this business has been rather a strain. Have you thought of taking a holiday?'

'Harriet and I had been thinking of going down to see her parents in the country for a week or so.'

He spoke as if he had heard nothing of what I had been saying earlier, as if he had prepared his own little speech and was going to carry on with it as if I hadn't had this outburst. 'I think that might be an excellent idea. In the meantime, you know you can always come and talk to me. We all have doubts, Richard, every one of us.'

The Article in the Newspaper

I opened my copy of *The Independent* the following morning to a terrible shock. There was a photograph of me outside St Michael's on the home news pages, and a long article. But it was the headline that horrified me: CHRIST IS MYTH, SAYS HACKNEY VICAR.

How could this have appeared without my knowing? I looked at the byline: Kevin Brown, the journalist from the Hackney Gazette. Clearly his ambition knew no bounds, and he had already moved on to higher things. He had recycled the information from our previous interview, the news story and my editorial, and woven this around the mysterious murder and the missing body. I suppose, for a piece of journalism, it was not too sensational, but I had no doubt that other papers would pick it up, and what they would say did not bear thinking about.

In the article Brown had also spoken to one or two people in the congregation who said unfavourable things about me. Only Tessa had 'declined to comment'.

Even as I read the article the telephone rang. Harriet, looking flustered, picked it up. She murmured once or twice and then waved at me, pointing to the door to indicate that I should go and take it in the other room.

'It's the Bishop,' she told me.

My mouth felt dry and I found it hard to speak. We have a new Bishop in Stepney, Hugh Martineau, and I had only met him once. I found him rather formidable.

'Richard Page here.'

'Hello. I've just seen this article in the paper. Not very pleasant, is it? I was wondering if you would like to come over and discuss it with me.'

We arranged to meet that afternoon at five. No sooner had I hung up than the phone rang again. This time it was ITV. Did I want to appear on tomorrow's London Programme? By lunchtime I had heard from Radio Four, the *Daily Mail*, the *Church Times*, the *News of the World* and BBC Radio London.

I patiently told them all that I would have to consider the matter carefully, and rang the London Diocesan Communications Officer, Andrew Sargeant, for his advice. He had seen that morning's *Independent* and thought that I should be very clear what I wanted to achieve if I was going to appear. 'If you leave it, the whole thing will probably blow over,' he said. 'There is a risk that the more you appear in the media, the more you will stir things up. It depends on whether you want this to happen, of course. It's nice to have religion in the public debate, but all publicity isn't necessarily good publicity for the Church.'

What did I want? My instinct was to say no, to leave things alone. On the other hand, it seemed to me that this was a very real chance to raise the question of what, in today's church, one was expected to believe, and that people didn't have to stay outside the church just because they couldn't swallow the whole of the creed. It was also perhaps a chance to clear my name.

I told him I would think about it and hung up. Some time ago I would have said I would have prayed about it, but this was now beyond me. I would talk to Harriet, and then, later, to the Bishop. Perhaps he would give me guidance.

✝he Bishop of Stepney

I felt unaccountably alarmed as I drove eastwards. I was penetrating deeper into the East End, into areas I didn't know, which still held for me an air of mystery. Of course, I was nervous. Although I knew that the Bishop was basically a traditionalist, I had heard enough of him to know that he was a warm and tolerant man. I suppose it did cross my mind that I might be in real trouble, that, if it came to it, I might actually lose my job. This didn't worry me too much. The Bishop could not expel me from the church, could not stop me being a priest. The very worst he could do was take away my licence to preach at London Fields, but there would still be hope of getting another job, perhaps in a parish under a more liberal bishop. After five years in London Fields, this might not be such a bad thing. But I didn't want to think of it this way. I thought that this was an ideal opportunity for me to explain my feelings, hopes and fears, to explain the situation honestly, to ask for his help.

I drove along Roman Road, straight as a die, and finally turned right at St Stephen's Road, Bow. I turned right again and then left in front of a grim, bricked-up warehouse and passed under an iron bridge. To the right, opposite a dreary modern estate, stood the gloomy Victorian Gothic residence, like something out of a Hammer horror film, with creeper climbing up one side and dark, unreflecting windows. I parked the car in front of the estate opposite and looked across the road.

In my anxiety not to be late I had arrived early. I sat in the car, fretting, messing with the car radio. At 4.55 I got out, walked up and down the road, and then nervously went up to the gate. As I walked up the path I saw a child's face peer momentarily out of the big bay window to the left.

There were no flowers in the garden, only some lugubrious laurel bushes under the window. The black door was sunk back inside the Gothic porch, and to the right was a little white bell.

The door opened before I could ring it. Somebody, probably the little girl, had told them I had arrived. The Bishop stood in front of me in his purple clerical shirt, holding his hand out in greeting.

He showed me through into his study. He pointed towards a high-backed, dusky pink chair in the corner.

'Sit down, sit down, how good of you to come. What would you like . . . some tea, some coffee, a little drink, not to inebriate, you understand, but to relax you . . .'

'Tea would be perfect.'

He went out for a moment. I glanced round the room. It was full of dark, Victorian furniture and lined with books. There were icons on the walls and I couldn't help noticing, to my right, a huge black-and-white photograph of what I could only assume to be Haile Selassie, crowned and holding the orb and sceptre. He had a thin, ascetic face, not unlike . . .

My thoughts were interrupted by tea arriving on a tray. The Bishop placed the cup and saucer on the table next to me. He noticed me looking at the photograph and said, by way of explanation, 'The Emperor, on his wedding day. Splendid, isn't it?'

I knew very little about Haile Selassie, except that he had been Emperor of Ethiopia and that the Rastafarians revered him as an incarnation of Christ. This did not seem to me a good omen.

The Bishop sat in a leather armchair opposite me, and gazed ahead, at the icon of the Trinity.

'I have read your letter in your parish magazine,' he began. 'There is nothing that I would take issue with there. But I think that you must be very careful what you say in public. It's all too easy to be misrepresented by the press.'

I said that I understood this and that I would be careful.

'However, I believe that this statement you made has

arisen out of other events in your church . . . events that are rather disturbing, and which have divided your congregation. Now, you know my role as a bishop is a delicate one. Of course I am anxious to support you vicars in your work, but I also have a responsibility towards the health of the whole Church...'

I said, 'I'm afraid it is more complicated than you think. I am not sure how you will take it . . .' There was nothing to be done but take the plunge. I began to explain what had happened, haltingly at first, but then in more detail. The Bishop sat very still, looking ahead of him, his hands on his lap, the fingertips pressed together. I told him about the sightings in the park, even told him about going to the man's flat, but when it came to it, I simply said that he had taken off his shirt and that I had seen the scars, and didn't mention the prostitute. Somehow, this last detail was beyond me.

When I finished he didn't say anything at first, sitting there deep in thought.

'Well?' I burst out, unable to wait any longer. 'Do you think I'm going mad?'

He smiled at me and waved his hand dismissively. 'Has anyone else seen this man? Has anyone else recognised him as the Christ?'

'Oh, he exists; I mean, he is not an apparition. As far as I know, it's only Mary, Mercy, a man called Gordon, and myself who have seen the resemblance . . . no one but me has seen the scars.'

'I see.' The Bishop looked ahead of him, at the beautiful icon. 'Well, I think I shall be guided spiritually in this.

No, I don't think you are going mad. I think I would feel if there were something narrow, obsessive, disturbed in what you say or the way that you have said it . . . but I think on the contrary that you are very honest, and that you are trying to make sense of something which seems beyond your normal experience. Perhaps this experience may prove fruitful, for yourself and for others in your church.'

The phone on his desk suddenly rang. He did not look up, but simply waited, and after four rings it was picked up elsewhere in the house. He picked up his teacup and drained it; I realised that I too had completely neglected mine, and that the tea had gone cold. I sipped it reluctantly, down to the bitter dregs.

There was a knock on the door and a woman put her head round. She said, 'It's a journalist from *The Times* . . . he says it's very urgent.'

The Bishop stood up and picked up the phone from his heavy, mahogany desk. He listened for a minute or so in silence. Then he said, 'Yes, I do indeed . . . well, I shall watch the community with great interest. Yes . . . you can say, "Isn't it wonderful that owing to this event, people in this community in London Fields are being challenged to think about their beliefs, and may be brought nearer to seeing Christ in everyone . . ."'

He looked up at me from the desk. He smiled, half-winked at me, and an expression almost of glee crossed his face. 'Yes, splendid. Thank you.' He hung up. 'Right, that's fixed him,' he said, coming back to sit opposite me.

His confidence with the press had impressed me; I saw at once that this was necessary, and that I would never be able to put up such a performance. I decided to ring up and say that I couldn't do the London Programme broadcast.

'But what do you think?' I asked again. 'Do you think it's a hallucination?'

'There is a difference,' he said, 'between a hallucination, which comes from your own mind, and a vision, which comes from outside. Besides, you told me that other people had seen this man.'

'Yes . . . that's true.'

'Then how can it be a hallucination?'

His eyes looked directly into mine. I felt a sudden, cold shock go through me. He did not think I was going mad; on the contrary, I think he envied me. It seemed he thought there was nothing strange about the idea that a resurrected Christ should suddenly pop up and start walking around the heart of Hackney, made obvious to those who were open to seeing him.

The Intruder

When I got home at seven Harriet was waiting for me. I knew at once that something had happened because she looked very agitated and her face was rather pale.

'Did you get on all right?'

'Yes, it was fine, he was very understanding . . . What's the matter, Harriet?'

'You didn't leave the chain on the door and go out the back way, did you?'

'No. Why?'

It seemed that when she had got back from a friend's house with the children at about half past six, she had not been able to get in through the front entrance because the chain was across the door. She had thought at first that I must have come back and she was frightened because she thought that things might have gone very badly at the Bishop's and that I had locked myself in. She went round to the back, but found everything was locked up and there was no sign of anyone. In the end she only got in by 'borrowing' a ladder from the neighbours and climbing up to the open bathroom window.

Now she thought there had been an intruder, because there were muddy footprints on the floor of the living room and some things had been curiously disarranged.

I went into the living room. Sure enough, there were muddy footprints, and some of the furniture had been moved. I went into my office. Papers had been moved from the desk and left on the table, and some of the books on the bookshelves were out of order. It was almost as if someone had been in the house searching for something, but failed to find it and left empty-handed.

I went through all the papers in the drawers of my desk, checking that nothing was missing. Then I went upstairs to tuck the children in.

'Was it a burglar, Dad?'

'He didn't take any of our toys.'

They were both very excited and it took a while to calm them down and get them ready for bed.

When I went downstairs Harriet said she supposed we should call the police. I said that I saw no point in it, as nothing had been taken and we didn't even need a crime number for the insurance people.

But Harriet wanted to call them; she was nervous, and quite frightened. 'What is going on, Richard?' she asked me.

I felt a sudden anger harden and tighten inside me. I began to wonder if I had not somehow stumbled on some kind of conspiracy. Perhaps Stone was right, and there really was something going on inside the church. Or perhaps there was some other meaning to it, something even worse, outside my experience, which I couldn't even begin to grasp.

I was not ready to accept that something supernatural was going on. A reincarnation of Christ did not burgle houses and leave muddy footprints on the floor. If Christ were to return to the world, surely there must be some point in it, some purpose, some message he was trying to put across. He wouldn't simply wander around Hackney fucking prostitutes and eating fish and chips.

No; there was a reasonable explanation somewhere, and I was going to get to it. I resolved to do something about it the very next day.

In a new mood of confidence I phoned the researcher on the London Programme and told her I would appear on their show the following night.

✝o Bart's Again

In the morning, after breakfast, I went to my office and cancelled my appointments. Of course I knew that there was a very real possibility that I was going mad, that I was having hallucinations, and that I had imagined something that wasn't there, but this explanation didn't satisfy me. It occurred to me that I could take someone else with me, someone objective, outside the church, to try to verify what I had seen, but this was impossible, because I didn't think that anyone else would ever entertain it. It meant entering the man's flat, forcing him to undress; how could I possibly do this? I could try again to tell the police and get them to question and examine the man, but I now distrusted the police and disliked Stone in particular so much that I could never do it; besides, they wouldn't listen to me. I also knew that I couldn't hand this unknown man over to the police. He might be an illegal immigrant, in which case he might be arrested or deported; whoever he was, I had no reason to put him in jeopardy to prove that I was sane.

Second, there was the possibility that someone was deliberately trying to deceive me, had arranged this whole thing as some form of mental torture, but that seemed too close to paranoid thinking to offer any comfort. There was Detective Chief Inspector Stone's theory, that this was a conspiracy within the church to fabricate a miracle, which gave me no great comfort either. Then there was the possibility that something supernatural really had happened. If so, I would be able to prove nothing. The whole point about the supernatural is that it can't be scientifically tested.

But finally, there was some tiny possibility that nagged at my mind. Was it possible that the man had not actually died? Could he have been pronounced dead in the hospital, taken off the life support systems and placed in the mortuary, only to recover and leave the hospital, perhaps with loss of memory caused by the lack of oxygen to the brain? But then there was the post mortem; no one could have survived that. Unless there had been a mistake and the post mortem had been carried out on the wrong body. Surely this was possible? But then, where had the scars come from?

Every so often one reads about cases of hospital mistakes, of people being given the wrong babies, having the wrong leg removed, having operations which were meant for someone else. Once I read a terrifying headline which said that every year 1,900 people die from unnecessary operations. Medical procedures and doctors are not perfect. Perhaps here, by some series of unlikely but possible coincidences, lay the clue to this mystery.

I went home and fetched my jacket, pausing to look at myself in the mirror in the hall. Was I imagining it, or had my hair gone greyer already? I pulled at the hair on my temples. I looked pale and unwell. The thought came into my head: You are going to die. Of course we all know that, at one level, but this time I felt I really understood for the first time that it was true. I was really, inevitably, going to die. I pushed the thought away, not wanting to dwell on it; I must suggest to Harriet that we go away as the Archdeacon suggested.

I combed my hair and straightened my collar. Then I took the car and went down to Bart's.

It was silly to go without an appointment, but I felt I couldn't wait. I asked if the senior registrar I had seen before, Mr Hunt, was there and was told he was in theatre, but would be out at noon. I asked if I could have an urgent appointment to see him. Again, the dog collar helped. The receptionist asked me to come back at two-thirty.

I wandered out of the hospital and walked aimlessly through Smithfield, looking at the huge carcasses of meat on display; then I sat down at a small drivers' cafe on the other side of the market and had a coffee. At two-thirty I was back at the hospital. Hunt came to see me in a room which was probably reserved for giving bad news to relatives. He was still wearing his operating greens and looked very puzzled to see me.

I thought I had better just come out with it. 'I know that what I am going to say will seem strange, but I'd like you to answer my questions, no matter how odd they seem.'

Hunt seemed unimpressed; he glanced down at his watch. 'I haven't got long, but I'll help you if I can.'

'Is it possible for someone to be pronounced dead when they are still alive?'

He looked at me in puzzlement for a few long minutes. Then he said, 'I remember you now. You came in to enquire about the man who died of knife wounds, about a month ago, the one who disappeared from the mortuary.'

'That's right.'

'Did the police ever find the body?' He paused, then smiled, and a look of something like impudence crossed his otherwise immobile face. 'He hasn't turned up again, has he?'

His eyebrows had shot up almost into his hairline. I couldn't help smiling. The honest way he gave voice to what no one else would mention cheered me, as a child's fear often vanishes when it is named. For the first time in a long while I felt quite normal.

'Please, just answer my question first.'

'Well, as you are probably aware, there is a whole protocol we have to follow in the event of a person on life support being thought to be brain dead. In this instance, as I recall, we had a man who was admitted with no blood pressure, severe bleeding from the heart, pulmonary artery and other vessels, and who had experienced a respiratory arrest. We had him ventilated at once but it's not clear for how long he hadn't been breathing. Following the operation he failed to breathe or show any other signs of life. It seemed pretty certain to me then that he was finished.

'If you're really interested, what we do is this. When we suspect someone has suffered brain death, which is, incidentally, final and irreversible, we have to have two doctors carry out a series of tests. These tests have to be carried out twice with a reasonable interval between, in some cases as long as twenty-four hours. We test for the absence of any reflexes, such as the corneal reflex, the gagging reflex, where we pass a tube into the windpipe to see if the patient responds, and the vestibular-ocular reflex, in which we pass two mils of ice-cold water into the auditory meatus and look for any eye movements. We also test for any response to pain. We then remove the patient from the ventilator for long enough to establish that the breathing reflex does not occur when the level of carbon dioxide in the blood rises above the level which would normally trigger it. If all these things are negative on two separate occasions, as certified by two doctors, then the patient is pronounced dead and disconnected from the life support systems.'

'Do you carry out a brain scan?'

'In these circumstances a brain scan is not considered necessary. It might be done if there were any doubt about the diagnosis.'

'Were you one of the two doctors who carried out the tests?'

'I was one of the two doctors. Believe me, he was dead.' Hunt got up from his desk and went over to the window. 'And if you are thinking there is any way it might be wrong, you also have the post mortem to consider. It was carried out on police orders on the Saturday, I believe, before the body disappeared.'

'Is there any chance there could have been a mistake there? That they could have done the post mortem on the wrong body?'

'I believe that the police also have a very strict protocol to follow. You could ask at the city mortuary and they might be able to tell you what the system is.'

I stood up and he opened the door. 'Now tell me,' he said, 'I've told you what I know, now you must tell me your end of things. Has he turned up, or what?'

'No, the body was never found.' I felt I had to say something more in explanation. 'We priests think so often of the spiritual side of death that we sometimes neglect to think of the physical realities. What you have said has been very helpful to me. I am very grateful to you for giving me your time.'

I went back to my car and made my way to the mortuary.

There Can Be No Doubt

I climbed up the concrete steps to the coroner's office and rang the day bell. The coroner's officer was there and let me in, taking me into his office and sitting down at his desk.

I explained my concern that there might have been some confusion about the body. I said that I knew this was unlikely, but that I wanted him to explain to me the procedure, so that I could be sure there had been no mistake.

The coroner took a deep breath, swivelling round in his executive chair. 'In the event of a violent death, there will be a police officer there on duty at the hospital. When the patient is pronounced dead, the body will probably be kept on the ward for the relatives to view and it will then be brought down to the mortuary. If it is a suspicious death, in this case, I believe you said, a murder, then the post mortem will be done here. The body will be transported here from the hospital in an ambulance and there will be a police officer in attendance.

'The police officer will formally sign the body over and may return after the post mortem is done to view the body and ascertain that the post mortem has duly been carried out on this same body. After that the relatives usually arrange for the undertaker to collect the body. We do all this so that there can be no possible doubt.'

'Do you remember the man who died on Easter Sunday from knife wounds? The one whose body disappeared the next day?'

He looked at me curiously. 'Yes, I do. We've had to review our security arrangements. Someone is coming to see me about that this very afternoon.'

'Is there any way I could find out who the police officer was who signed the body over?' A suspicion had come unbidden into my mind. Once you suspected corruption in the police force, there was no limit to where this could lead. If Stone could suspect me, then surely I could suspect him.

He said, 'I could probably look up the records for you. Please wait here, and I'll go and see.'

He was gone for perhaps ten minutes. I sat in the office, patiently waiting for him. I realised as I sat there that I had been expected to attend a meeting at the priory that afternoon and would simply not have turned up.

Once again I was neglecting my duties; almost certainly I was having a breakdown. I put my face in my hands.

He came back into the room. 'It was a Sergeant Black from Stoke Newington Police Station. But in fact, I should have told you at the outset, I was present at the post mortem. I know that it was the same man who came in, whose picture was in the papers, who the sergeant signed for. I was there and saw it done. So you see, there can be no doubt.'

I looked at the man, at his solid, reassuring manner, and wondered, as I have often wondered before, how people can do such jobs. I thanked him and left the building. Outside, it had started to rain. People were scurrying backwards and forwards in the unexpected downpour, holding jackets or waterproofs over their heads, running for cover. I stood there for some time, bewildered, not knowing what to do. The trail I had been following had come to an end. There was no explanation. It was as if a giant hole had appeared in the ground before me, opening up a new vista into which I didn't dare look. It was as if everything I had based my life on, everything I had taken to be true and solid, had dissolved away before me. It was not as simple as a revelation that there was no God. Perhaps it was a revelation that there was a God, and that he worked in ways I could not imagine, and I, through my own weaknesses and fears, could not believe that his purpose was a benign one. I tried to bring myself back to reality, to decide what I had to do. Then I remembered with sudden horror: I was supposed to appear on television that night. I had to get a number 55 bus. I could get to the priory for the end of the meeting. I would ring the television people and say I was ill, and go to ask the doctor to put me on tranquillisers. I would ask Harriet to take us away for a few days.

I put up my arm to shield my face from the downpour and made a run for it across the road. The noise of the horn and the screeching of brakes were blurred into one sound for me as I saw the taxi and felt the impact, and then suddenly everything was darkness.

✝he Brush with Death

They told me later that I only lived because an ambulance was close by when they called 999. They were there within a minute. In less than three minutes I was on the stretcher and within fifteen in the operating theatre. They said that the operation took three hours and that they transfused thirty litres of blood because the liver had been damaged and the liver loses a lot of blood. I was in a coma for three days and in intensive care for a week and remember very little about any of it.

What I do remember very clearly is that shortly after I was admitted to hospital I had what is known as a 'near-death' or 'out-of-body' experience.

I have a vivid recollection of a body lying on an operating table. I could see the doctors and nurses, the urgent looks on their faces, people shouting and people running. I viewed this scene from the top left-hand corner of the room, tucked in somewhere near the ceiling. The ceiling was very high and seemed to fade into a pale, blue-green haze, similar to the colour of the surgeon's operating gowns.

I could hear, in this dreamlike memory, very faint music playing. The music was very high, not quite like anything I have ever heard. The nearest would be the high female voices in a Russian Orthodox church singing from behind the rood screen. I came in closer to the body on the table and could see that it was me. The abdomen appeared to be split open and there was an awful lot of blood.

I felt anxious in this memory when I recognised who I was seeing, but not very anxious. After this I studied the faces of the doctors and nurses around me. I can still see them clearly.

Later, when I was a little better, I asked two doctors to sit down and take detailed notes of my descriptions of the people who were working on that body. The doctors checked the records to find who had been in that team and the descriptions were very accurate. They both agreed that there was no way I could have been conscious or otherwise known who had been there, and they didn't seem to consider very seriously that somebody had set this up. They said my experience was a classic one and decided to pass this on to some organisation which was carrying out research into near-death experiences.

There is one final part of this dream or memory, I don't know what to call it. After the memory of the operating table I felt as if I were being propelled along a dark corridor to a bright light at the end, like being in a railway tunnel when the train lights are out and seeing the daylight shining enormously bright at the other end. I wanted desperately to reach this light, like a drowning person trying to break the surface of the water. I am not saying that this proves that there is life after death. Perhaps, on the contrary, this 'tunnel of light' is some distant memory of being born. I am quite prepared to believe that at the moment of death or near-death there are processes which occur in the brain which give rise to visions or hallucinations, and I am also prepared to believe that there may be a moment of super-consciousness before the system finally shuts down.

There is another strange thing which I am told is fairly common. After I came from surgery and was in a coma I was aware of Harriet's presence, even when they thought I was unconscious. It was simply the feeling that when Harriet was there everything was all right and when she was absent it was not. It is similar to the feeling I had that when I believed in God everything was all right and that when I had lost my faith everything felt wrong.

I felt safe when Harriet was there because I knew she would protect me, because I was afraid then that they would pronounce me dead. I thought that they could perform all those tests and that I would be aware of them and feel pain, but not be able to move or rouse myself.

My injuries were fairly serious. I had a ruptured liver,

which had caused most of the bleeding, a fractured pelvis, and both legs had been broken in several places. My skull was also fractured. At first, when I regained consciousness, I had no memory at all of the accident, and this caused Harriet a lot of pain, because the taxi driver had sworn to the police that I had seen him coming, had stared right at him, and had thrown myself in front of him deliberately.

I could not remember ever having seriously contemplated suicide, though in moods of deep depression I suppose I had sometimes thought about it, wondering what it must feel like, for example, to jump from Beachy Head, and whether you would regret what you had done halfway down. But such had been my state of mind in the days and weeks leading up to the accident that I couldn't dismiss it as a possibility. Harriet, then, was left at my bedside for several weeks, believing that she had failed me and that she and the children meant so little to me that I didn't want to live.

✝he Psychiatrist

After I moved out of intensive care and began slowly to recover, they sent a psychiatrist to see me. He was quite a young, good-looking man, and he seemed to have unlimited amounts of time. He asked me about my childhood, my mother's death, and of course was fascinated to discover that this was by suicide. He kept asking me how I felt about these things, as if anything which I could put into words could reflect the agony which I had felt. He kept saying, 'We have to sort this out. We can't have you going home until we've found out what really was behind this... you may need a little bit of help.'

At first his approach irritated me, so I argued with him. 'I'm not sure that I did want to kill myself. Anyway, even if I did, I am very glad to be alive. I don't think that it would happen again.'

'What reasons do you have for feeling that?'

Everything with him was answered by a question. In a way it was exhausting, though in time I came to look forward to his visits as a break in the boredom of the hospital routine. At first I was rather cautious about what I told him. I was happier talking about my childhood than about the present. But one morning when he came to sit down beside me, as usual holding the file with my notes – which I would have loved to have had a chance to glimpse – I decided to tell him about my experiences with the man who had died.

I suppose I had hesitated to at first, for fear of being thought to be schizophrenic or psychotic, but gradually he had gained my trust. He listened to me with fascination. Later, he told me how Jung believed that man had an innate religious sense, and that ideas of God came out of archetypes – the wise man, the saviour, the virgin, the mother – which we all held deep within our minds. We all had these archetypal images, and sometimes we projected these on to people around us, imbuing them with qualities which they, as mere mortals, couldn't possibly have, and this inevitably led to disappointments when they let us down.

As we talked, I began gradually to feel that I understood at last what had happened to me. Over the last few years, I had been slowly renouncing my faith, moving steadily towards the rationalist position that Christianity was a myth, a myth which held important lessons for us all, but a myth none the less. But emotionally I was not ready to accept this. The tragic loss of my mother and the presence of a father who cared for me only in a cool and distant way had created in me a desire for unconditional love from somewhere else, together with a deep desire that the wrongs I had suffered would eventually be put right. So strong was my inner need for this personal God, the Christ of faith, the worker of miracles, that I had created him out of my imagination, and projected him on to this poor young immigrant whose face was sufficiently like that of Jesus to accept him.

The Recovery

As I became physically stronger, and as talking to the psychiatrist began to allay my fears, I slowly began to regain my peace of mind. I found how delightful it was to do nothing, and that hours could be happily spent studying the contours of a bunch of flowers, reflecting on the infinite shades of colour in one lilac stem, or studying the reflection of sunlight on the curtain. I now think that the accident was the best thing that could have happened to me, despite all the distress that it caused Harriet and the children. Perhaps in a way I did die, and was reborn.

Bit by bit the world seemed to become a little more real to me. People were very kind and came to see me constantly. They brought me books to read, magazines, tempting morsels of food. Harriet took a month off work and was with me every day from twelve thirty till three, when she went to collect the children from school. When she could she came back in the evenings. She used to sit by me, telling me anecdotes about people in the parish, reading me stories, or just sitting in silence, holding my hand.

Towards the end of my stay in hospital, Tessa came to visit me. She told me that she had met a divorced man twenty years older than herself, that she had fallen in love, that they were getting married and that she was expecting a child. Tessa was forty-two and had never imagined that she would be a mother. She looked radiant and incredibly happy. She told me that she didn't know any more if she wanted to be a priest and I told her I was sure this was the best thing.

She took my hand and squeezed it. 'I'm so glad that what happened that day did happen,' she said to me. 'It was only when it all came out into the open that I realised I was wasting my time thinking only of you. In a way, it set me free. Thank you.'

✝he Prostitute's Flat

Some time after I was well again and back at work, I decided to go back to the house in St Mark's Rise. I wanted to finish off this 'unfinished business', and I went now not in a spirit of dread or obsession, but simply to find out the truth about the young man who had been the object of my obsession. I rang the bell and the girl I had seen on my previous visit opened the door. She looked very surprised when I said I wanted to talk to her and invited me into her flat.

She was dressed in casual clothes and wore no make-up, and looked as if she had put on weight. She put the kettle on and sat down at the table. 'Well,' she asked me, 'what do you want?'

'The man in the top flat . . . is he still there?'

'He left a month ago.'

'Do you know where he's gone?'

'He didn't leave an address.' She didn't seem anxious or suspicious of my questions, just answered matter-of-factly.

'So there's no way I could trace him? I wanted to write to him.'

'I don't even know his name.'

This shocked me for a moment, but then I realised that she must have so many clients that she couldn't possibly remember their names. On the other hand, this wasn't just a client, he lived in the same house, and there had been something intimate about their coupling; I felt they knew and liked one another. 'I thought he was your . . . boyfriend.'

'Oh, well, we did, you know, do it a few times.' She looked at me and grinned. 'I feel silly, really, saying that to a vicar.'

'Not at all.' The kettle had boiled; she got up and made me a cup of tea. It was cheap, bitter tea, which left a deposit on your teeth, and we drank it out of grimy cups.

'I wanted to write to him. You see, I recently had a very bad accident, I nearly died, and I believe he had also been in a bad accident . . . he had terrible scars.'

Now she did look at me a bit oddly. She said, 'He had a heart operation. He told me. He nearly died. It wasn't in this country, it was where he came from, somewhere odd, you know, one of those new countries that used to be in the Soviet Union.'

When I heard this I felt as if something had fallen into place. Relief flooded over me; I felt released. Perhaps there had indeed been a rational explanation for everything. I told her that if she heard from him I would like to talk to him and gave her my number at the church. I finished my tea. Just as I got up to go, she put her hand on my arm, and said, 'You know, he was the best thing for me. There was something about him. It was because of him I kicked the habit. He had this funny effect on people. He just looked at me, you know, and he said, "You don't want to be doing that." And suddenly I didn't, and I stopped, just like that. I'm not on the game any more, either. I've got myself a job, and I'm getting my daughter out of care.'

✝The Reckoning

I was sitting in my office at night, the lamp shining on my desk, the cross on the window ledge shining dully in the dimness. I was writing in my notebook. I was trying to make sense of everything that had happened, was trying to record it, perhaps as a book.

I paused before picking up my pen. The only thing that still bothered me was the missing body. That, out of everything that had happened, was inexplicable. Or was it? Stone had showed, on reflection, a remarkable lack of interest in following up the case, except for throwing wild accusations at me or at my congregation. There had been something odd about his behaviour from the beginning. It occurred to me that I might have been deliberately set up. It was possible that this man had been a terrorist, an assassin or a spy, involved in illegal business in London. Perhaps he was involved with secret arms deals for some new Middle Eastern state; one certainly read enough about such things in the papers. That would fit with the lack of identification on the body, and the fact that no one had ever claimed it. If MI5 had removed the body, or if it had anything to do with any of the intelligence services, then there was certainly no way that the truth would come out. Even the police might be told nothing, except perhaps a nod and a wink not to pursue the case any further.

Everything that had happened had been the result of a series of extraordinary coincidences. That was obvious. Had the death taken place at any other time and in any other place no one would have thought twice about it. It was clear that on that day, in the Good Friday service, I had been highly suggestible. My overcharged emotions had led me astray, into magical and irrational thinking.

And this is very odd, when you come to think about it. There must be some reason why these potent myths still exercise so much power over us. The most real thing we know about the life of Jesus is his death. We know, because it is recorded in other works of history, that he was crucified under Pontius Pilate, dead, and buried. Because he died we know that he must have been born, but otherwise we know very little about him. From recent historical research, we can be fairly certain who he was, one of many itinerant Jewish teachers of the time, in contact with the Essene monasteries perhaps, preaching the message of salvation and the imminent coming of the Messiah. Perhaps he was just a good man, inspired and eloquent, trying to make a better world. He believed, like others, that there are spiritual rather than just material values and that if we can live by faith we can make things better. While we throw out all the other beliefs, about heaven and hell, the end of the world and the second coming, the resurrection and eternal life, we can still go on with that.

I picked up my pen and began to write. As I did so, I became aware of a faint noise inside the church. There was the sound of something banging, something being dropped, someone moving about. Instinctively I felt in my pocket for the keys. They were there, and the church was locked. I thought rapidly. Surely a burglar couldn't have got in without some breaking glass? Could someone have picked the locks? I had better investigate.

I meant to get to my feet and go to look, but I didn't. I have done the same thing when woken in the night, hearing a sound which might have been a burglar, knowing that I won't be able to sleep until I've gone to look but unable to tear myself out of bed and do so. So I sat, pen poised, and listened.

I could hear footsteps, quiet but distinct, crossing the church floor. They came to the door, and then I heard them continue, without the tiniest pause, along the corridor. There is a door between the church and the corridor, and I knew it was locked. I had locked it myself, not half an hour ago, after locking up the other side of the church and checking all the lights were off.

I knew that something strange was happening, but this time I was not afraid. Rather I felt excited, expectant, and for some reason the light in the room seemed to become brighter and clearer, as sometimes happens when you are very tired and your perceptions seem to alter, as if you were calling up some extra resources from the brain. I didn't look up from my desk, but I knew that somebody was there, had come into the room, and I could hear behind me his quiet, steady breathing.

Nothing moved. There was a long, long silence in the room.

His voice came softly, caressingly, out of the darkness. He said, 'I believe you have been wanting to speak to me for some time.'

Also available from
WWW.MAIAPRESS.COM

Merete Morken Andersen AGNES & MOLLY
£9.99   ISBN 978 1 904559 28 3

The story of two friends and the man they both desire. When he asks Molly to take care of his two children, Agnes is jealous. She comes to help, and a real struggle for power begins, with the women battling for the affections of the children. A richly atmospheric novel about friendship, jealousy and love.

Merete Morken Andersen OCEANS OF TIME
£8.99   ISBN 1 904559 11 5 | 978 1 904559 11 5

A divorced couple confront a family tragedy in the white night of a Norwegian summer. International book of the year (*TLS*), longlisted for The Independent Foreign Fiction Prize 2005 and nominated for the IMPAC Award 2006.

Michael Arditti GOOD CLEAN FUN
£8.99   ISBN 1 904559 08 5 | 978 1 904559 08 5

A dazzling collection of stories provides a witty yet compassionate and uncompromising look at love and loss, desire and defiance, in the 21st century.

Michael Arditti A SEA CHANGE
£8.99   ISBN 1 904559 21 2 | 978 1 904559 21 4

A mesmerising journey through history, a tale of dreams, betrayal, courage and romance told through the memories of a fifteen-year-old. Based on the true story of the Jewish refugees on the SS *St Louis*, who were forced to criss-cross the ocean in search of asylum in 1939.

Michael Arditti UNITY
£8.99   ISBN 1 904559 12 3 | 978 1 904559 12 2

A film on the relationship between Unity Mitford and Hitler gets under way during the 1970s Red Army Faction terror campaign in Germany in this complex, groundbreaking novel. Shortlisted for the Wingate Prize 2006.

Booktrust London Short Story Competition
UNDERWORDS: THE HIDDEN CITY
£9.99   ISBN 1 904559 14 X | 978 1 904559 14 6

Prize-winning new writing on the theme of Hidden London, along with stories from Diran Adebayo, Nicola Barker, Romesh Gunesekera, Sarah Hall, Hanif Kureishi, Andrea Levy, Patrick Neate and Alex Wheatle.

Marilyn Bowering WHAT IT TAKES TO BE HUMAN
£8.99   ISBN 978 1 904559 26 9

The day after World War II is declared in Canada, Sandy Grey attacks his father for refusing to let him sign up. Incarcerated in an asylum for the criminally insane, he has to find a way to survive and convince his doctor that he is truly sane. Dramatic and lyrical, rich and strange – this is no ordinary thriller.

Hélène du Coudray ANOTHER COUNTRY
£7.99   ISBN 1 904559 04 2 | 978 1 904559 04 7

A prize-winning novel, first published in 1928, about a passionate affair between a British ship's officer and a Russian emigrée governess which promises to end in disaster.

Lewis DeSoto A BLADE OF GRASS
£8.99   ISBN 1 904559 07 7 | 978 1 904559 07 8

A lyrical and profound novel set in South Africa during the era of apartheid, in which the recently widowed Märit struggles to run her farm with the help of her black maid, Tembi. Longlisted for the Man Booker Prize 2004 and shortlisted for the Ondaatje Prize 2005.

Olivia Fane THE GLORIOUS FLIGHT OF PERDITA TREE
£8.99   ISBN 1 904559 13 1 | 978 1 904559 13 9

Beautiful Perdita Tree is kidnapped in Albania. Freedom is coming to the country where flared trousers landed you in prison, but are the Albanians ready for it or, indeed, Perdita? 'Thoughtful, sorrowful, highly amusing' (*Times*)

Olivia Fane GOD'S APOLOGY
£8.99   ISBN 1 904559 20 4 | 978 1 904559 20 7

Patrick German abandons his wife and child, and in his new role as a teacher encounters a mesmerising 10-year-old. Events begin to spiral out of control – is she really an angel sent to save him?

Maggie Hamand, ed. UNCUT DIAMONDS
£7.99   ISBN 1 904559 03 4 | 978 1 904559 03 0

Unusual and challenging, these vibrant, original stories showcase the huge diversity of new writing talent coming out of contemporary London.

Helen Humphreys WILD DOGS
£8.99   ISBN 1 904559 15 8 | 978 1 904559 15 3

A pack of lost dogs runs wild, and each evening their bereft former owners gather to call them home – a remarkable book about the power of human strength, trust and love.

Linda Leatherbarrow ESSENTIAL KIT
£8.99   ISBN 1 904559 10 7 | 978 1 904559 10 8

The first collection from a short-story prizewinner – lyrical, uplifting, funny and moving, always pertinent – 'joyously surreal . . . gnomically funny, and touching' (Shena Mackay).

Kolton Lee THE LAST CARD
£8.99   ISBN 978 1 904559 25 2

H is a boxer past his prime, dragged into a gunfight in a gambling shebeen and then into debt to a sinister sociopath. He must face his demons and enter the ring one last time. A striking noir thriller set on the meaner streets of London.

Sara Maitland FAR NORTH & OTHER DARK TALES
£8.99   ISBN 978 1 904559 27 6

Tales drawing on classical mythology and tradition from every continent, revealing the dark and bloody side to many familiar legends. The title story is a major film starring Michelle Yeoh and Sean Bean, directed by Asif Kapadia.

Sara Maitland ON BECOMING A FAIRY GODMOTHER
£7.99   ISBN 1 904559 00 X | 978 1 904559 00 9

Fifteen new 'fairy stories' by an acclaimed master of the genre breathe new life into old legends and bring the magic of myth back into modern women's lives.

Dreda Say Mitchell RUNNING HOT
£8.99   ISBN 1 904559 09 3 | 978 1 904559 09 2

A pacy comic thriller about Schoolboy and his attempts to go straight in a world of conflicting loyalties, bling and petty crime. An exciting debut, winner of the CWA John Creasey Award in 2005 for best first crime novel.

Vigdis Ofte & Steinar Sivertsen, eds. VOICES FROM THE NORTH: NEW WRITING FROM NORWAY

£9.99   ISBN 978 1 904559 29 0

A rich and compelling anthology of work, both prose fiction and poetry, by leading young Norwegian writers, published to celebrate Stavanger as a European Capital of Culture in 2008.

Maria Peura AT THE EDGE OF LIGHT

£8.99   ISBN 978 1 904559 24 5

A girl growing up in the far north of Finland experiences first love, sex, obsession with death, tension within her family, and a desperation to leave the restricted life of an extraordinary and remote community.

Anne Redmon IN DENIAL

£7.99   ISBN 1 904559 01 8 | 978 1 904559 01 6

A chilling novel about the relationship between a prison visitor and a serial offender, which explores challenging themes with subtlety and intelligence.

Danny Rhodes ASBOVILLE

£8.99   ISBN 1 904559 22 0 | 978 1 904559 22 1

Young JB is served with an ASBO and sent to work on the coast. Frustrated and isolated, his growing feelings for Sal offer a chance of rescue, but a storm is coming that threatens to shatter his hopes. A moving and atmospheric debut.

Diane Schoemperlen FORMS OF DEVOTION

£9.99   ISBN 1 904559 19 0 | 978 1 904559 19 1   Illustrated

Eleven stories with a brilliant interplay between words and images – a creative delight, perfectly formed and rich in wit and irony.

Henrietta Seredy LEAVING IMPRINTS

£7.99   ISBN 1 904559 02 6 | 978 1 904559 02 3

Beautifully written and startlingly original, this unusual and memorable novel explores a destructive, passionate relationship between two damaged people.

Emma Tennant THE FRENCH DANCER'S BASTARD

£8.99   ISBN 1 904559 23 9 | 978 1 904559 23 8

Adèle Varens is only eight when she is sent to live with the forbidding Mr Rochester. Lonely and homesick, she finds a new secret world in the attic – but her curiosity will imperil everyone, shatter their happiness and send her fleeing, frightened and alone, back to Paris. An intriguing modern take on Brontë's masterpiece, *Jane Eyre*.

Emma Tennant THE HARP LESSON

£8.99   ISBN 1 904559 16 6 | 978 1 904559 16 0

With the French Revolution looming, little Pamela Sims is taken from England to live at the French court as the illegitimate daughter of Mme de Genlis. But who is she really? 'Riveting and very readable' (Antonia Fraser)

Emma Tennant PEMBERLEY REVISITED

£8.99   ISBN 1 904559 17 4 | 978 1 904559 17 7

Elizabeth wins Darcy, and Jane wins Bingley – but do they 'live happily ever after'? Reissue of two bestselling sequels to Jane Austen's *Pride and Prejudice*.

Norman Thomas THE THOUSAND-PETALLED DAISY

£7.99   ISBN 1 904559 05 0 | 978 1 904559 05 4

Love, jealousy and violence in this coming-of-age tale set in India, written with a distinctive, off-beat humour and a delicate but intensely felt spirituality.

Karel Van Loon THE INVISIBLE ONES

£8.99   ISBN 1 904559 18 2 | 978 1 904559 18 4

A gripping novel about a refugee in Thailand, in which harrowing accounts of Burmese political prisoners blend with Buddhist myth and memories of a carefree childhood.

Adam Zameenzad PEPSI AND MARIA

£8.99   ISBN 1 904559 06 9 | 978 1 904559 06 1

A highly original novel about two street children in South America whose zest for life carries them through the brutal realities of their daily existence.